AF351892

SAVING THE SUNSET BAR AND GRILL

By Margaret Magle

Four Windows Press

Sturgeon Bay, Wisconsin

Copyright © 2017 by **Margaret Magle**

All rights reserved. No part of this publication may be reproduced, distributed or transmitted in any form or by any means, without prior written permission.

Margaret Magle/Four Windows Press
231 N. Hudson
Sturgeon Bay, WI 54235

Publisher's Note: This is a work of fiction. Names, characters, places, and incidents are a product of the author's imagination. Locales and public names are sometimes used for atmospheric purposes. Any resemblance to actual people, living or dead, or to businesses, companies, events, institutions, or locales is completely coincidental.

Saving the Sunset Bar and Grill/ Margaret Magle. -- 1st ed.
ISBN 979-8-9905946-7-8

Dedication

Saving the Sunset Bar and Grill would not be possible had it not been for the encouragement and support of my friends and family.

Thank you to my beta readers Laurel, Nicole, Barb, and Robert.

Thank you to Barb for helping me with all my technical questions and also my beautiful cover.

Big thanks to Thomas Davis who agreed to take a chance on me.

And I would never have a book finished if it wasn't for my husband, David, who took over the household chores and the snuggling duties of our cats so I could spend my time writing.

Contents

CHAPTER 1 1

CHAPTER 2 5

CHAPTER 3 7

CHAPTER 4 9

CHAPTER 5 13

CHAPTER 6 17

CHAPTER 7 19

CHAPTER 8 21

CHAPTER 9 25

CHAPTER 10 33

CHAPTER 11 35

CHAPTER 12 39

CHAPTER 13 43

CHAPTER 14 47

CHAPTER 15 51

CHAPTER 16 55

CHAPTER 17 61

CHAPTER 18 65

CHAPTER 19 71

CHAPTER 20 75

CHAPTER 21 79

CHAPTER 22 81

CHAPTER 23 85

CHAPTER 24 87

CHAPTER 25 89

CHAPTER 26 93

CHAPTER 27 97

CHAPTER 28 101

CHAPTER 29 105

CHAPTER 30 107

CHAPTER 31 111

CHAPTER 32 115

CHAPTER 33 119

CHAPTER 34 125

CHAPTER 35 129

CHAPTER 36 133

CHAPTER 37 135

CHAPTER 38 139

CHAPTER 39 143

CHAPTER 40 147

CHAPTER 41 149

CHAPTER 42 151

CHAPTER 43 153

CHAPTER 44 159

CHAPTER 45 161

CHAPTER 46 165

CHAPTER 47 167

CHAPTER 48 169

CHAPTER 49 173

CHAPTER 50 177

ABOUT THE AUTHOR 179

CHAPTER 1

"Beth, you look amazing," Annie said, straightening the hem of Beth's black sequined floor length gown. "Terry is going to take one look at you and ask you to marry him all over again."

"I hope so," Beth replied, looking at her reflection in the mirror, touching the auburn curls which Annie had so carefully created to accent the backless gown. Beth also couldn't help but notice the glint of several grey hairs beginning to show around her face.

"That was a rather large sigh," Annie said, pushing up from the floor, "Tell mama Annie what the problem is."

"I don't know. It's probably me being crazy, but it seems like Terry and I are not on the same page anymore."

"How's that?

"He spends so much time at work the past few months, late at night too. When he is home, he is thinking about work, or researching for work, or talking on the phone to someone about work."

"You said it yourself; he has a few major cases coming up," Annie said, resting her chin on Beth's shoulder, looking at her in the mirror. "That's gotta make your man awfully tense."

"Maybe you're right," Beth said, not very convincingly. "He did make dinner reservations tonight. I cannot remember the last dinner we went out to that did not include one of his colleagues or a client."

"I bet you a free manicure there will be no talk of work tonight when he sees you dressed like this," Annie said with a laugh, as she started to clean up her workstation. "I'll even throw in a pedi if you get a little somethin', somethin' extra tonight. If you get my meanin."

"Oh, I get your meaning."

"If my Darian saw me in that dress, we wouldn't be havin' dinner out."

"That is also something Terry has not been too interested in either lately."

"Blame it on the work; you're still young married people. How long has it been now, 22 years?"

"This is the big 25."

"That is a good long time. Hell, that's twice as long as I put in with all three of my husbands combined. In my book, you got a good thing goin' for yourself."

"Perhaps that is the problem. It has been too long. What if he is tired of waking up every morning to a 40 plus, greying hair, no longer 36-24-36 wife?"

"Ain't never gonna happen, Beth Campbell," Annie said, "Look at yourself. You are beautiful and loving and sweet and…"

"Stop it," Beth said with a smile.

"You stop it. Stop worrying." Annie reached for the broom and began sweeping the loose hair on the floor. "I think Terry has been puttin' in all this overtime to impress the big wigs at the firm. Pretty soon they ain't gonna have a choice but to add his name to the letterhead.

"I can see it now - Perez, Browne, and Campbell Law Firm. Soon you'll be ridin' in a white limo, shoppin' at all the high-class boutiques in Denver like Neiman Marcus and Nordstrom's. Get your spa treatments at some la dee da salon with pink champagne and embroidered fuzzy robes."

Feigning a pained look on her face and rolling her eyes, Annie continued much to Beth's amusement, "Then you will forget all about poor little Annie Howard, your best friend since diapers, slavin' away at Clippers 'R Us for minimum wage plus tips."

"Now that is something that ain't never gonna happen," Beth replied, her smile genuine. "I would not trust anyone else to make me look this beautiful." Beth fluffed her curls with both hands.

"Ha!" Annie said, pointing at her friend, dustpan in hand, spilling the freshly swept hair back onto the floor, "You admit that you are beautiful."

"Only because of your hard work. Speaking of work, I think your next client is here," Beth said as the little silver bell above the door rang.

"I hate keeping old Mrs. Wagner waitin'," Annie said, tucking the broom and dustpan into the cabinet. "She tends to get a bit cranky."

"Knock 'em dead tonight," Annie said, giving Beth a quick hug. "I never asked where you are going tonight."

"We are having dinner at Frasca's and then seeing The Black River Orchestra. Fourth row, center."

"Those are the hottest tickets in town. How'd you score 'em?"

"Terry settled a nuisance suit for the owners of the theater. They said 'anytime,' and Terry took them up on the offer."

"See, the perks are startin' already."

Beth flashed a quick smile Annie's way as her friend disappeared around the divider.

"I'm just going to use your phone," she called out. "I forgot to charge mine before leaving home."

"Just leave a dime on the counter," Annie called from the next room.

"You have reached the confidential voice mail of Terrance Campbell, at Perez and Browne. I am either…"

Beth didn't wait to hear the rest of the all too familiar message and instead pressed 0.

"Perez and Browne Law Firm, how may I direct your call?"

"Hi Marie," Beth replied, "Is my husband around? I tried his desk."

"I'm sorry, Mrs. Campbell," Marie said, haltingly, "Didn't you get my message?"

"I do not have my phone with me. What message?"

"Mr. Campbell and Mr. Alverez were called in for a last-minute meeting. I'm not certain, but I have a feeling it will be a long one."

"Why do you say that?"

"I was asked to call in a double order of sesame chicken and all the sides from Mandrin Connection. That's not a good sign. Did you want me to get a message to your husband?"

Beth sighed.

"No, that is fine," Beth answered, feeling anything but fine. "Have a good weekend."

"You too, Mrs. Campbell," Marie replied. "Oh, and Happy Anniversary."

Beth put the receiver back on the cradle. Another sigh. Beth realized she had been sighing a lot lately. Slipping her jacket over her shoulders, she stepped out of the salon and hailed a cab.

CHAPTER 2

The first thing Beth noticed when she stepped out of the cab was the lights were on in the townhouse. Perhaps Marie had been wrong about the marathon meeting and Terry was dressed and waiting for her to come home. Maybe the meeting was a ruse, and he was planning to surprise her.

"Hello?" Beth called out entering the living room. "Terry, are you home?"

No answer.

Beth set her purse on the glass-topped end table and walked toward the kitchen. Her face lit up when she saw the tall crystal vase on the center of the table. She approached slowly, counting the number of blue shaded roses in the vase. Twenty-five. One for each year. She was a little impressed that Terry had remembered how long they had been married. Beth opened the silver envelope attached to the vase and read the card.

Dearest Beth,
Thank you for the 25
wonderful years together
Love always, Terry

Beth sighed and tipped her head back, fighting the tears beginning to form. Two things gave the flowers away as not being Terry's idea. First, during all the years they had dated and then been married, Terry had never called her 'dearest'. Second, the card had been filled out in Marie's perfect flowing handwriting.

Letting the tears flow freely, using the back of her arm, Beth sent the vase flying across the room. She watched as vase and flowers crashed into the ivory, tiled wall. The trail of water mirrored her tears, leaving a rose filled puddle on the kitchen floor.

CHAPTER 3

Beth kept playing the last day's events over and over. Getting 'beautified' as Annie called it. Going home to a lit but empty house. The flowers. The mess of shattered glass, water, and roses strewn on the kitchen floor. Then the hurried, frantic packing. More crying. Finally, the metallic 'chink' of her wedding rings hitting the closet door. Why she hadn't left them behind was a mystery, but they were now hanging on a gold chain around her neck. The other item not left behind was the black evening gown. There was the temptation of leaving it spread out on what had been her side of the bed with a note saying, 'See what you missed,' but instead, she had carefully packed the dress in the garment bag and it and the other three matching suitcases were now in the trunk and back seat of her car.

Her car.

Beth exhaled.

Her car. A bright yellow 1978 VW bug she had purchased from a pair of brothers the summer after high school. It had been her first adult purchase. Paid for from her after school and weekend jobs at Mustard's Last Stand and The Frosty Cow ice cream stand. Terry barely tolerated Betty, the name Beth had christened the car with, when they were dating. As things became more serious, Terry insisted on driving anytime they went anywhere. Once married, Betty was relegated to a garage stall under a tarp. Beth would take her out once or twice a month whenever Terry left on a business trip. She always made sure the tarp was back in place by dinner times on Sunday.

There were many times Terry had threatened to sell the 'eyesore', but thankfully some work crisis would sidetrack him, and the discussion would be tabled for a while. Annie had promised if Terry carried out that threat, she or one of the members of her large extended family would buy the car and keep it safe.

CHAPTER 4

When she had left Boulder, the sun was nearly set. Driving at night was never her issue. There was less traffic which provided fewer distractions and allowed her to think. The problem nagging at her was where she planned to go. One option was Seattle; she had friends from college there, but that would mean turning around and heading northwest. San Francisco would have her backtrack. Her aunt and a few cousins who lived in Nashville, Indiana. She remembered how small and quiet that town was, bigger than Nederland, but still small. Saint Louis was an interesting place, but it also was a place Terry had family. That made it out of the running for sure. New Orleans? Great food, but Terry connections again. For someone who was used to planning everything out, not knowing what to do was annoying. Spontaneity was not one of her strong suits.

Beth wiped her eyes with the heel of her hand. She had been on the road for over 8 hours and been awake for 12 hours before that. The air conditioner on full and the radio blasting 80's rock music did little to keep her awake. Six cans of caffeinated soda followed by energy shots had long passed their effectiveness. She could have found a hotel along the way, but sheer determination kept pushing her forward. Her last bathroom break and refreshing walk had worn off somewhere around Grand Island, Nebraska, and she was beginning to rethink her no hotel idea. Up ahead, Beth could see what appeared to be a multi-colored hot air balloon hovering next to the interstate ahead of her. As she drove closer, she saw that the balloon was in fact a water tower indicating York, Nebraska. Maybe there would be a hotel or at least a truck stop. Beth smiled when she spotted the lit sign proclaiming Petro Truck Stop. Beth drove into the parking lot and parked Betty under a light post. She reclined her seat and covered herself with a blue travel blanket.

Beth slept for only a bit over three hours, but the sleep produced an odd and enlightening dream. There had been trees, lots of trees. A curvy road and lots and lots of water. It all seemed so familiar; Beth swore she could smell a campfire. After breakfast at the truck stop, a shower and change of clothes, Beth bought and filled an insulated cooler bag with a cold roast beef sandwich, a bag of chocolate covered potato chips, gummy bears, a six pack of soda and and a pair of energy drinks. Her smile was a genuine one as she thought of Annie. Her friend had always said, 'road trip food should look like a ten-year-old packed lunch.' With the exception of the sandwich, this bag would meet Annie's approval. By the time she had finished the first soda, Beth's mind and memory had cleared and she knew just where to go. It was a place even Terry would not think of. This is where she would drive to and think about what to do next. Beth programmed her phone app to give her directions to Ellison Bay, Door County, Wisconsin.

She remembered, vaguely, spending time at her great grandparent's cabin in Ellison Bay. She had been seven years old the last time she had been there. What she remembered most was the trees and the outdoor bathroom. There was a proper bathroom with a shower in the house, but grandpa still used the outhouse and had it cleaned out once a month. "Tradition," he would say. "Plain German stubbornness" Beth's mother would say. That summer, at age seven, would be the last time Beth and her parents would visit the cabin. Great grandpa Arndt died that winter, and her mother died the following summer.

Beth's father never left Colorado after that. He hermited himself away in their cabin in Nederland. Beth had spent more time with Annie's family than at her house. The year she left for college in Boulder was the last time she saw her father. He died that October. Beth met Terry that December at college when she stayed in the dorms over Christmas vacation. It was shortly after that when she moved into his boyhood home and from there to the townhouse.

This trip was one of the few times Beth had ever been really alone. And, surprisingly, free.

Beth continued thinking about the family cabin during the rest of the drive, which had become much more pleasant as she thought about her destination. There were more bathroom breaks and stops along the drive, and these were not as hurried as before the dream stop. Beth ate her sandwich and took pictures of the four art pieces located at an overpass near Omaha. More pictures crossing the Missouri and the Mississippi Rivers. Coffee break in Council Bluffs, Iowa where the landscape was hillier than the rest of her trip so far, and the landscape was dotted with wind turbines.

Next stop would have to be Des Moines for much needed gas and a decision. Beth could either continue on I-80 and pay tolls or cut north and head towards Dubuque and, soon after, the border to Wisconsin. With the jingle from the Dubuque Ham commercial going through her head, she headed north to Wisconsin, closer to her destination.

CHAPTER 5

Beth had been driving for about six hours when she came to a terrible realization, two of them. One was that the gas gauge was entering the dangerous red zone, and the second was that she was hopelessly lost. She had found her way easily to and through Madison, only getting caught circling the capital building twice before getting into the correct lane leading out of the city. A few miles out of Sun Prairie, road construction had forced her to detour. She was so far off the path. the phone app map that she had laid out in the morning no longer made sense. Added to that was the fact that her phone was out of power, so even doing a corrected app was impossible.

After a few more miles of driving, Beth spotted a brown Wisconsin map-shaped sign which read, Rustic Road next 15 miles. She was too annoyed for not having filled up the car when she stopped for a sandwich, her only thought was the hope that a rustic gas station would appear along the rustic road. Beth didn't have to wait long. After two more curves, the trees became sparse and opened into fields followed by an intersection. On one corner was an old wooden white church with a sign reading, Services Sunday 10:00 and 3:00 and 'Bread and Soup fundraiser Saturday at 5:00'. There was a cemetery across the street surrounded by a wood and stone fence. The third corner held a dilapidated bench and a rusty phone booth, minus phone. The last corner housed a two-story tavern. The exterior needed a good paint job, and the extra wide steps leading to the porch sagged in the middle, and, thankfully, in front of the porch, a single gas pump. Now, if only the pump worked, Beth thought to herself.

Even before she had completely pulled up to the pump, a boy, no more than ten or eleven, came bounding down the steps and stood next to the gas pump, a big, genuine smile on his face.

"How much you want?" he asked, still smiling.

"Just fill it up please," Beth replied. "Do you take credit cards?"

"Nope, just cash," the boy replied, "There's a machine inside."

Beth could tell the boy's smile had faded to a questioning frown that he had not seen too many cars like Betty.

Beth opened the luggage compartment in the front of the car and unscrewed the gas cap. The boys' smile returned as he began filling the car with gas.

Beth had run the air conditioning in the car, and that was a distinct difference between the car's interior and the oppressive humidity outside. Nevertheless, it felt good to be out of the car and walk around a bit.

The inside of the bar was not much cooler than outside. Several large ceiling fans were fighting to circulate the air a bit. Several of the patrons turned in her direction but most merely continued to talk and drink their beers. Beth caught sight of the cash machine squeezed between an antique juke box and a popcorn machine. Country music was playing from the juke box, and over the music Beth could hear sounds of an arcade machine and pool balls clacking together coming from a side room. Beth punched in her code and requested $80.

When Beth turned back toward the bar, the boy was seated on a barstool, and she could hear him excitedly talking to the bartender, who was his grandfather, about the yellow backwards car outside.

"The gas will be $42," the bartender said, looking away from his grandson. Beth handed him three of the crisp 20's. The bartender made change from a cash register, which looked as though it was from the same era as the juke box. She took the bills and gave $5 to the boy who smiled, hopped off the stool and ran to show the tip to the men playing pool.

"I think you made his day," the bartender said. "Most people just grumble about the prices and drive off. Can I get you a drink?"

"No thank you," Beth replied. "What I could use is a place to charge my phone so I can get directions back to the highway."

"Let me see the phone."

Beth handed her phone to the bartender who quickly found the correct cord and plugged it in. He bent down behind the bar and came up with a bottle of root beer in one hand and a paper map in the other.

"Drinks on me. It's a sticky one out there. Where ya headed?"

"Ellison Bay," Beth said taking a sip of the cold soda

"Door County, pretty easy drive from here," he said, unfolding the map and pointing to a large red arrow drawn on the map. "This is us, and this is where you want to be. You want a sandwich or something for the trip. Dotty made fresh chicken salad this morning."

Thinking it would be polite to at least order something in return for the man's help, she agreed. Beth also took a candy bar out of the box on the counter which stated it was a fundraiser for a band trip.

While waiting for the sandwich, Beth asked to use the bathroom. That request would give her phone a few extra minutes to charge. When she came back to the bar, there was a brown paper box on the counter and another cold root beer. Looking at the receipt, Beth took another candy bar from the box and set her last $20 on the counter.

"Just keep following the highway until you get to Green Bay and turn off toward Milwaukee. After you get over the bridge it is a pretty straight shot. Once you get to the Door, if you get lost again, you're bound to hit water eventually. Hope you have a room ready there. It is tourist season startin' up."

Beth thanked the man again and took her phone, which had a bit of a charge at least, and headed toward the door. She stopped in the open doorway when the bartender called out, "It's only a few hours' drive but you better hurry. There's weather comin' in. Dotty's knees are telling her it's gonna be a big one."

Stepping out of the door and looking at the dark gathering clouds to the north and west of her, she knew he was right.

CHAPTER 6

The bartender had been right. The directions were easy to follow. However, once she passed the large wooden Welcome to Door County sign and the 10-foot-tall cement mouse pointing north, large raindrops began to beat down on the windshield. Remembering back to her 8th grade science class, large raindrops like these were often followed by hail. Thankfully no hail yet. By the time she had passed over the bridge on the outskirts of Sturgeon Bay, the rain was whipping, and it took all of Beth's concentration to see the white stripes on the center and sides of the road. The high winds beating against the car only made driving more difficult. Lightning lit up the sky, followed quickly by loud, booming thunder as she passed through the small town of Jacksonport. By the time she reached Baileys Harbor, her wipers were nearly useless against the downpour.

As the bartender had predicted, rooms were not going to be easy to find. Neon signs flashed 'No Vacancy' or sometimes the more polite "Sorry".

It was shortly after the sign indicating 'Sister Bay 5 miles', the car started to shutter and threaten to stall. Beth looked to the gas gauge; still more than ¼ tank. The service engine flashed on, and Beth could feel a lurch as the car lost power for an instant and then started again.

"Oh Betty, not now," Beth pleaded. "Come on sweetie. You can make it."

The car lurched again as lightning flashed and thunder boomed around her, echoing across the water.

"Don't you do this. We are almost there."

Beth slowed for another curve, and the car sputtered again. This time she could feel the car slowing down and stalling with no hope of revival. Beth turned the wheel hard right and pulled into what she hoped was a parking spot by the side of the road.

Frustrated from the drive and the car's betrayal, Beth gave in to her emotions. Letting out a large sigh of resignation, she folded her hands on the steering wheel. Thunder continued to roll overhead. By the time her head fell in place on top of her hands, Beth had already fallen into an exhaustion-fueled sleep.

CHAPTER 7

Beth jolted upright. As her head cleared, she realized the rain had stopped, and the thunder rumble was far off. Nothing in the car was disturbed, and the doors were still locked.

She blinked her eyes, trying to figure out what had woken her up. Then Beth became aware of voices and footsteps outside the car. She blinked again as a beam of light flashed outside the window.

"Miss," a male voice said from behind the light, "Are you OK?"

"Are you all right?" a second man asked.

"Please step out of the car so I can see if you are hurt," said voice one.

Beth felt for the car's door handle; her eyes still not focusing from the flashlight glare. She opened the door slowly and stepped out, her body ached all over.

"When the neighbors called in saying there was a car in my front lawn," man two said, "I expected a drunk tourist who had lost his way."

"My car stalled," Beth managed to say softly.

"Are you hurt?" man one repeated.

Beth rubbed her eyes to focus, grateful the flashlight was now pointed in a different direction, and she found herself face to face with two rather large men. At 5-foot 1 inch, she felt small and insignificant next to them. One was dressed in a fitted brown uniform with a badge and name tag reading, C. Neuville. He was the one holding the flashlight. The other was holding a smaller flashlight and wore jeans, a blue t-shirt and tennis shoes.

"I think I'm ok," Beth said, finding her voice, "My car stalled, and I could not see the road."

The shoulder mic on C. Neuville's shoulder beeped.

"Go ahead and answer it," Number two said, "I'll handle our little criminal trespasser myself. She doesn't seem too dangerous."

Beth watched as the sheriff car disappeared down the road and around the curve heading back into Sister Bay.

"You look exhausted. Are you staying close by?"

"I was trying to find a place when the car stalled."

"Without a reservation? Good luck with that. It is the start of tourist season up here after all."

"So, I have heard," Beth said with a sigh.

"Well, have no fear, I know a place that keeps a room open for just such an emergency.

"By the way, I'm Marcus Reed, rescuer, at your service."

"Beth. Beth Campbell."

"Well Beth, Beth Campbell, what do you need for the night? I can grab it and take you next door. We can get the rest in the morning."

Beth reached into the back seat for her suitcase and handed it reluctantly to Marcus, still unsure of this situation. The first drops of rain began again as she reached in the front seat for her keys and purse.

Marcus grabbed her hand with his free hand and began running in the direction opposite her car as the rain poured down on them. He helped her up the three steps of a large house. The sign next to the door read "The Rose Garden Bed and Breakfast". Marcus pulled a key from his pocket and unlocked the door.

"Welcome to Door County." he said as a peal of thunder echoed in the sky.

CHAPTER 8

Beth woke up feeling the warm sun on her face. She lay there for a few moments, comfortable on soft pillows, the scent of roses filling her nose. Not opening her eyes, she reached an arm to her left where Terry should be but only felt pillows, and soft fur.

"What the...?"

Beth sat up and opened her eyes. Looking to her left she saw a fluffy grey cat jump off the bed and hide under the large wooden dresser on the opposite side of the room. This was not her familiar tan bedroom with clean white dressers and matching king-sized bed with white padded headboard and grey bedspread. Instead, she was on an intricately carved four poster bed with lace curtains and a pale pink comforter with tiny pink rosebuds. The walls were a darker shade of pink. The floor next to the bed had a soft green rug. Swinging her legs off the bed, she sunk her feet into the rug, the pile caressing them.

Beth stood up and looked around the room. There was a door off to the right side of the dresser. Another door was on the left. This door was slightly open, and she could see it was a bathroom. Underneath the window was a low table, cherrywood Beth guessed by the color, which was the same wood as the dresser and bed. An antique rocking chair with a quilt draped over the back sat in a corner opposite. There was also a small nightstand with a lamp and several books and a small basket containing assorted candies in red and white striped bags labeled Confectionary.

Catching a glimpse of herself in the large wood framed mirror over the dresser was all Beth needed to bring herself back to reality. Her rumpled clothes and hair that looked as though the grey cat, still peeking out from under the dresser, had made a bed in it. Her purse was hanging from the doorknob of the left-hand door. Beth opened the door and found her single suitcase inside. Her shoes from last night were on the floor of the closet. Maybe she really had been so exhausted from the drive she didn't remember finding a vacancy, checking in, and pouring herself into bed.

Taking the suitcase to the bed, she pulled out a tan skirt and blue two-piece sweater set with tiny flowers which matched the flowers at the hem of the skirt. Getting another look at herself in the mirror, Beth grabbed her hairbrush and make up bag from the suitcase. She chose a pair of large bath towels and a washcloth from the table and stepped into the bathroom. The deep rose colored clawfoot bathtub called to her, but she decided on the shower instead.

The pulsating water felt good on her sore muscles. There was a transparent rose-shaped soap in the soap dish and small bottles of fruit scented shampoo and conditioner on the shower shelf as well. Beth watched the whirlpool of water bubble down the drain, washing the grime, soap suds, and a great deal of pent-up anger wash down with it. As the water beat down on her body, everything over the past days came back to her again. The drive, getting lost, the rain, the car breaking down, and the man bringing her here. What was his name? Matthew? Mitchell? No, Marcus. Had he taken off her shoes and put her to bed? What else did he do?

No! She was not going to be negative. He seemed very nice last night from their quick encounter.

Beth went back into the bedroom and dressed. She combed the tangles from her hair and pulled it back into a loose braid. Her legs were still smooth from the spa treatment two, or was it three, days ago, and she switched out the more stuffy and proper nylons and pumps for a pair of sensible sandals.

After putting her suitcase back in the closet, Beth carefully pulled the sheet and comforter up and plumped the pillows, placing them neatly at the top of the bed propped against the headboard. Whenever she had stayed at a hotel with Terry, she would straighten the room, separating the garbage from recycling, and putting the wet towels in the tub. Terry would berate her by saying, "That's what the staff gets paid to do".

"Terry!"

Under a second window was a desk and matching cushioned chair. There was a green shaded desk lamp and an old dial telephone. She smiled, thinking just how appropriate that was for this room.

Picking up the receiver she began to dial the phone, hoping to be able to make a long-distance call. She listened as the phone rang through on the other end.

"Hello," came a familiar voice, "You have reached the home of Terrance and Beth Campbell."

Beth didn't bother listening to the rest of the message. If the machine was picking up, Terry was not home. Had he ever come home? Did he see the mess? Did he realize she had left? Most of her things were still there. Did he care?

She didn't take much time to dwell on her problems. The loud growl in her stomach told her it had been a very long time since she had eaten anything but a sandwich and chocolate bar. Picking up the phone again, she dialed another number. This time the answering machine message consisted of three children's voices.

"Annie, it's me. Sorry I didn't call sooner, but my phone ran out of charge. I am fine. Don't worry. I will explain when we can talk to each other. Love you girl."

Beth's stomach rumbled again. She opened the heavy door and went into the hallway. Faint piano music and laughing could be heard from downstairs. The smell of bacon and fresh baked bread wafted up the stairs, sending Beth's stomach into yet another series of hunger rumbles.

A grey streak beat Beth down the steps and disappeared.

CHAPTER 9

The staircase going downstairs dominated most of the front hallway. A curve at the bottom opened into a wide hallway. Crisp white and pink lace curtains accented the many windows of the entrance hall. She could see more of the same lace curtains. These, though, were floor-length, gracing the windows in the library/music room off to the side of the stairs. The focal point of the hall was a large front desk carved from the same type of wood as the staircase. A copper-colored plaque attached to the front of the desk proclaimed the house as The Rose Garden Bed and Breakfast, established 1984. The picture on the wall above the desk was that of a couple, the woman holding a baby girl who, Beth guessed, was about 6 months old. Both parents were looking down at the baby, and Beth could read the emotions of pride and love on their faces. Edna, Earl, and Rose Anderson were engraved in the gold metal oval under the picture.

More laughter and piano music came from the library room. There was a fire burning in the stone and wood fireplace which took up half of one wall. Two cornflower-blue overstuffed chairs sat in front of the fireplace, and a cream and cornflower braided rug lay in between the chairs. The grey cat, which had been in Beth's room earlier, was now curled on the rug. Both chairs were occupied: one was an older man who looked to be in his 60s and was reading a newspaper, and the other a girl who looked to be in her teens reading a book with a blue oriental dragon on the cover. The couple on the piano bench in front of an antique upright piano was the source of the laughter. She was desperately trying to play a tune from the sheet music perched on the piano. He was doing everything in his power to distract her - blowing on her neck, kissing her cheek, striking the wrong key - she would simply slap his hand away, and the laughing would begin again. On the other side of the room, two floor to ceiling glass doors led to an enclosed porch.

From where she stood, Beth could see a white tea cart with a pitcher of water and several glasses on top. There was also a large table with a puzzle on top. An older man was focused on the picture of a lighthouse on the box top and choosing pieces off the table in his effort to try and make them fit. He emitted a satisfying grunt with each located piece. Beth walked over to the puzzle table. The man looked up long enough to acknowledge Beth's presence before studying the box lid and pieces.

His search was cut short by the ringing of a bell coming from what Beth had guessed was the dining area, judging by what she had been able to see from the hall. All the other occupants of the room stood and headed towards the dining room, and Beth followed. She was greeted by a young woman in a blue dress covered by a white apron dotted with pink roses. Judging by the size of her belly, she looked to be around eight months pregnant, and when she moved, her face couldn't hide how uncomfortable she was.

"Good morning, everyone," she said. "My name is Samantha. Mrs. Anderson is busy with other business, and I will be your host this morning. Help yourself to breakfast; there is more of everything in the kitchen."

Of the twelve place settings at the table, only eight besides her spot were occupied.

The table was covered in a white cloth and matching white placemats. Mixed china and stoneware dishes were set on each placemat. Assorted glass and mismatched silverware were placed next to the dishes. The center of the table was covered with serving dishes full of food. Ham, fried potatoes, and scrambled eggs steamed in the bowls. Tiered silver stands on each end of the table held an assortment of breads and rolls. Several decorative jars of jam were scattered around the table. There were also two baskets on the table, one filled with red apples and the other with large navel oranges. Beth took a small amount of each item as it was passed around the table. As a bowl or basket was emptied, Samantha would take the dish, disappear for a few minutes and reappear with a full dish of food. Beth had to admit, this breakfast tasted much better than anything she had managed to cook at home.

"Would you like some coffee?"

Beth looked up, startled by Samantha's question.

"Or maybe milk?"

"Milk, please," Beth replied.

Samantha brought out a large glass of milk. Beth had managed one drink and another bite of the cheesy potatoes before a hand touched her shoulder.

"Well, good morning," a cheerful female voice said, "Marcus didn't want to wake me when he brought you in last night."

Beth looked up and found herself looking at an older version of the young mother in the photograph by the desk.

"Marcus brought the rest of your suitcases in early this morning after the rain stopped. He also asked me to give you this."

"Thank you, Mrs. Anderson," Beth said, reaching for her cellphone which was in the older woman's hand.

"Please, call me Edna, dear. Mrs. Anderson makes me feel old," the woman said with a laugh.

"Do you have my car keys?"

"I'm afraid not. Marcus said he was taking your car to the city to see what needed to be fixed," Edna said, shaking her head, "But don't worry, he knows a good shop to take it to, my dear. Your car will be good as new soon."

Beth sighed. She didn't like the idea of strange people driving or even touching her Betty.

Too many times, Terry had said he was going to send Betty to a shop, and when he had said it, she knew the car would not be coming back.

"There's nothing to worry about," Edna said, as if reading Beth's thoughts, "You can trust Marcus."

Beth was not fully convinced. All she knew of Marcus was the fact he was a stranger whose yard she landed in last night during a rainstorm.

During their conversation, the rest of the guests had left the table, some taking an extra roll or piece of fruit before leaving. She could hear them saying their goodbyes and thank you's as they left.

A bell began to ring from the kitchen.

"My pies," Edna said happily, "Please join me in the kitchen."

Beth followed Edna into the kitchen. She was immediately struck by the myriads of sweet and spicy scents. Edna handed Beth an apron that matched Samantha's, and she instinctively put it on. As Edna was taking a perfectly latticed apple pie from the oven, Beth had a chance to look around the kitchen. It was much different from the tiny and worn kitchen she had learned to cook in. The kitchen at the townhouse had been something out of an expensive showcase of homes. Shiny stainless-steel appliances and stuffy tiles. Even the decor on the walls was stiff and impersonal. This kitchen felt homey, the place where she imagined kids decorated Christmas cookies, and turkeys and lamb were carefully prepared for special occasions. The counters were lined with fresh baked goods. Two more pies came out of the oven, both just as perfect as the one Edna had just placed on the cooling rack. Parchment paper covered the center table and held a variety of cookies and muffins. There was also a pair of strange looking desserts, which, to Beth, looked like an oversized Danish but with a thick crust and topping of something that looked like a white cheese.

"Those are Belgian pies," Edna explained, noting the questioning look on Beth's face.

"This one is rice, and the other is prune. I make cherry and apple when the fruit is in season. Would you like to try some?"

Before waiting for an answer, Edna cut a thin slice from each pie and put them on a plate for Beth and handed her the plate and a fork. Beth had never had rice in a pie before, but she found the dessert very tasty. Tasting the prune-filled pastry, Beth wasn't sure what to think. But she did have to admit the breakfast today was much better than the bagel and coffee she swallowed down while trying to get Terry up and out of the house so he wouldn't be late for work after staying up until one or two working on a brief or opening statement. As Beth ate, Edna continued to fuss around the kitchen, finding baskets for the cookies and plates for the muffins and slices of pie.

"Did you have a chance to meet any of the other guests yet?" Edna asked, pulling yet another pie from the over.

"Not yet, but I did wake up to a grey cat on my pillow."

"Oh, that's Cleo," Edna said with a laugh. "He must have snuck in. He thinks he owns the place. Most of the guests have left already. Next weekend will be a busy one, though. Two festivals in the county and the cherry blossoms should be peaking soon. Those happenings always bring the tourists. Right now, we have the Culver's. We have Mr. Samuels and his granddaughter Emily, who come every year. The Blake's are newlyweds."

"They were the couple at the piano?" Beth stated more than asked.

"Yes," Edna said with a smile. "They have been here a week in the Orchid room. Mark my words, there will be a baby coming around in nine months."

Beth had to laugh, not expecting a comment like that coming from a sweet lady like Edna appeared to be.

"I've been in this business enough years to know things, if you know what I mean dear," Edna said, as if reading Beth's thoughts again.

"Cute couple," Beth said, taking a broken cookie Edna offered her.

"Snickerdoodle?"

"Who was that older man by the puzzle?"

Edna rolled her eyes. "That's Thomas; he is more pest than guest. He comes around once or twice a week and loiters at the puzzle table long enough to get a fresh donut or cookie."

"But you never ask him to leave, Edna, do you?" Marcus said, suddenly appearing and then bending to give Edna a kiss on the top of her head.

"Well, it's about time you came back," Edna replied, ignoring the question. "I was waiting for the lunch groceries."

"I had to stop and bring you these," Marcus replied, holding out a round glass bowl filled with colorful carnations. "After all, you are my favorite neighbor and innkeeper around here."

"Just set the flowers on the table and bring the rest of the groceries in," Edna said, turning so Marcus couldn't see her blush. She took the flowers into the dining room, leaving Beth and Marcus alone.

Marcus left out the screen door and returned quickly with several bags which he set on the counter. As he began unpacking the bags, separating the canned goods from the refrigerated items, Beth was able to get a look at the man who came to her aid last night. As she guessed last night, he was just over six feet tall. His hair was a medium shade of red with just enough grey-white streaks to make him look about Beth's age. His eyes were a bright green. He was clean shaven, something Beth had always thought looked better on a man. Like last night, Marcus was wearing well-fitting blue jeans and tennis shoes. His t-shirt, black this morning, was covered by a black leather jacket.

"Well, Beth, Beth Campbell," Marcus said, as he turned around and noticed Beth staring at him. "You look much better this morning than you did last night. Did you sleep well?"

"Thank you," Beth replied, feeling a slight warmth in her cheeks. "Edna said you took my car into the city. How did she look?"

"Better than my lawn," Marcus replied.

Beth lowered her head embarrassed.

"Actually, it's not as bad as it sounds," Marcus quickly added, "I was planning on tearing out that patch of grass sooner or later. You just helped make the decision sooner rather than later."

"Did you remember the meat from Jackie?" Edna asked, coming back into the kitchen, "She said it was all wrapped and ready for pick up."

"It's all in the chest freezer downstairs," Marcus answered, "and I remembered to stop in Carlsville for coffee and tea."

"What would I ever do without you?" Edna said, wrapping her arms around Marcus's waist.

Marcus returned the hug and again kissed the top of the older woman's head.

"I'll be back later to see if you need anything else," he said. "I have to pick Abby back up from the post office and make sure Aaron wakes up and comes over to help you today. Don't forget the meeting tonight at 7:00. It was nice seeing you again Beth."

"You, too," Beth answered, not turning away from the sink.

When she heard the screen door bang shut and a vehicle start up and drive away, she finally turned around, a slight blush still visible on her cheeks.

"He is quite handsome, is he not?" Edna commented, putting the canned goods into the cupboards.

"I had not really noticed," Beth answered, knowing it was clearly a lie. "I was just thinking about how I ended up in a room here last night. Did he…?"

"Oh no, my dear, Samantha heard Marcus bringing you in and helped him put you to bed. She took off your shoes and socks and covered you up. Marcus was a perfect gentleman, I was told."

Beth let out a sigh of relief. She wasn't really sure what she imagined happened but was happy to hear Edna's explanation.

"So does Samantha live here?"

"Only for a short time. She was afraid to be alone up on the Island so close to her due date. She and her younger brother both came early. Samantha said she wasn't taking any chances of her baby being born on a ferry crossing Death's Door."

Before Beth could ask for more of an explanation there was a bell ring from the front hall.

"Come Beth," Edna said, taking off her apron and straightening her dress. "We have guests."

Beth untied her apron, slipped it over her head, and placed it on the back of a chair.

"After we check in our visitors," Edna continued, "We can start straightening up and you can tell me all about how you ended up in Marcus' front yard in the middle of the night."

Beth sighed, something she realized she had been doing a lot lately. This was not a conversation she was ready to have with anyone except Annie just yet.

CHAPTER 10

Beth helped Edna check in a new pair of guests, the Marshalls from Minnesota, who were here to celebrate their 42nd anniversary. Edna explained they came here every year. They met one summer when they were both on family vacation. Even when the families no longer came, Edwin and Ruth kept in touch. Through phone calls and letters they fell in love.

When they were 25 and 22 respectively, they agreed to meet up at the Alpine Resort where they had spent their vacations. The night before they were set to leave, Edwin surprised Ruth by reserving a table on the upstairs porch of the Sunset Bar and Grill, a beautiful restaurant overlooking the bay. That night he proposed, and, obviously, she said yes.

Over the years, the Marshall family grew, four boys and three girls. They came on vacation to Door County as often as they could afford the trip. As the children married, and the grandchildren came along, the Inn was too small to accommodate everyone, but the family always made an appearance. Soon the children and grandchildren stopped coming, mostly because jobs took them too far away. But Edwin and Ruth kept coming back. It felt as though the family was still coming, however, through the pictures and cards that were brought along. Every May they made the trip, still as very much in love as the first time they came. On the last night of their trips, they would go back to the Sunset to commemorate the night Ruth said yes.

After she had finished with the story, Edna excused herself to go back to the kitchen and finish preparing the box lunches for the guests to take with them, if they liked, and make sure all was set for the meeting which would be held in the study later that evening. Samantha, who had finished cleaning up the dining room and breakfast dishes also excused herself and went to her room to lie down.

Now alone, Beth decided it would be a good time to stop putting off a phone call she needed to make.

CHAPTER 11

"But you're, ok?" Annie asked on the other end of the phone.

"More or less," Beth replied, using her foot to make the porch swing gently move up and back, "I am still trying to figure out what to do now."

"Where exactly did you land?"

"Wisconsin, Door County to be exact, if you must know."

"Where's that?"

"My mom explained it to me like this whenever we came to visit my great grandparents. Hold up your left hand; that's Wisconsin. Your thumb is Door County. Sister Bay is right around your fingernail."

"Why there?"

"I did not actually plan to come here, but somehow, it drew me in," Beth said. "I think partially because I remembered how peaceful the cabin was when I came as a child, and partially because I never told Terry about my visits here. One of the few secrets I kept from him."

"But you're, OK?" Annie asked again.

"Yes, I'm OK."

"And you have money and a place to stay?"

"Yes, mom!" Beth said with a laugh. "I took everything I could out of the savings account along the way. After the accident, I was put up in a very nice Bed and Breakfast run by…"

"Accident? What accident?" Annie asked, interrupting Beth's sentence. "You said you were OK. You ain't lyin" to me, are ya?"

"It was really nothing," Beth replied. "There was a storm when I arrived here, and Betty stalled out. When it stopped raining, I discovered I had crash-landed in someone's yard."

"But you're, OK?"

"Would you stop asking me that?" Beth said, laughing again. "The only things hurt were Betty, Marcus's front yard, and my pride."

"Marcus, who's Marcus?"

"The person whose yard I destroyed. He's the man who lives next to the Inn I am staying at."

"Is he cute?"

"I did not take the time to get a good look at him last night," Beth lied, not wanting to tell Annie he had come by this morning. She was also happy Annie couldn't see her blush. "It was dark and late, and I was really tired."

"Well, if he lives next door, you oughta run into him again I think."

"I have more important things to think about than some man next door. For example, where am I going to stay, and what am I going to do before my money runs out? It is not like Boulder or Denver where I can find a studio apartment to move into. And I am not sure there is much call for a freelance lifestyle reporter around here."

"You have other skills like organizer and party planner and babysitter. After all, you took care of my three monsters and survived," Annie said.

This time both friends shared a laugh.

"It's good to hear you laugh," Annie said, this time more seriously, "I can't imagine what you must've felt like that night. I knew Terry was a jerk sometimes, but not that kind of jerk."

Beth reached up to feel the wedding ring which was still hanging around her neck and let out a sigh.

"Hey, I didn't mean to bring ya down again," Annie said softly.

"It is not you," Beth replied, "I don't know what I was thinking. I was just so mad. Terry's worked all-nighters before. But I thought with dinner and a concert, that night would be different, special even. I cannot believe I was so stupid to think he had changed. Even if it was our anniversary."

"You're not stupid," Annie said. "Terry is the stupid one for not seein' the good thing he had in you."

"Thanks for trying to make me feel better, but I am still sitting here with no place to live, no job, not knowing anyone in a strange place."

"No one but Marcus," Annie teased.

Before Beth could get a word of objection out, she could hear a child's high pitched 'MOMMY' on Annie's end of the phone line.

"I gotta go before the beasts kill each other," Annie said over the children's screams.

"Call me tomorrow? I get out of the salon at five."

"I will. I promise," Beth said. "And thanks for listening."

"Any time, hon," Annie replied, "And I mean any time. Day or night."

"I love you; you know."

"I know. Take care, OK?"

Beth hung up the phone. One call down, one to go.

"You have reached the home of Terrance and Beth Campbell…"

Beth hung up the phone, put her head back on the porch swing, and for a few minutes, watched the white clouds float casually across the blue sky. Slowly she stood up and went back inside the Inn and up to her room.

CHAPTER 12

Beth blinked open her eyes and looked at the clock next to the bed. 7:25. After talking to Annie and coming in from the porch, Beth had returned to her room and found her suitcases neatly lined up near the closet as Edna had said. There was also a room key on the dresser. It was an actual key, not the plastic card she was used to seeing at hotels. This was a large metal key on a carved, wooden keychain, a painted rose rather than a number adorned both sides of the chain. Having only unpacked what was necessary, Beth changed out of her skirt and top and slipped into a comfortable pair of jeans and a knit blouse and lay down on the bed for a short nap. 'I was more tired than I thought', Beth said to herself. It was then she realized she was also hungry, breakfast and pie being over ten hours earlier. She hadn't even taken Edna up on the boxed lunches she had helped assemble.

Stepping out of her room, Beth could hear a loud variety of voices from downstairs and remembered Marcus had mentioned something about a meeting tonight at 7:00. Going down the stairs, she could tell the voices were coming from the large library room to the left of the stairs. People were milling around the main hall and ·lounge room where the piano was. More people were in the dining room, even out on the enclosed porch. From what she could guess, there seemed to be about 30 people, none of whom had been guests from this morning. And no one really seemed to pay much attention to her, a fact she was honestly grateful for.

Out of the corner of her eye, Beth saw Samantha enter the hall carrying a large silver tray loaded down with cookies and sweets from this morning's baking. Samantha looked even more worn out than she had this morning.

"Here, let me take that," Beth said, hurrying to Samantha, relieving her of the tray. "Where does it go?"

"Thank you," Samantha replied, breathing heavily, "This way."

She led Beth to the library and a wooden table which looked like a match to the breakfast table only twice as long. The matching chairs were placed around the room in a horseshoe pattern, two rows deep. More cushioned chairs and a few wooden folding chairs were set around the room.

Samantha indicated an empty space on the table for Beth to set the tray on. The rest of the table was filled with more small plates of pie slices and muffins, pitchers of water and milk, and urns for coffee. A young girl with long black hair and a boy who looked like a mini version of Marcus were gathering up empty glasses and mugs and heading out of the room. The boy gave Beth a questioning glance as he passed. Samantha picked up two water pitchers and handed them to Beth before picking up a coffee urn and went out into the hall and towards the kitchen.

"There you are," Marcus said, coming in from the porch carrying a bag of ice cubes. "Did you find the rest of your things? I left them for Edna this morning."

"Yes, thank you," Beth answered, not turning around from the sink where she was refilling the water pitchers.

"You need to add ice," Marcus said, placing the bag in the adjoining sink.

The sound of a plate hitting the floor caused Beth and Marcus to turn around to see Samantha trying to lift another silver tray off the counter, a plate and pie on the floor, and an empty spot where the plate had been on the tray.

"Aaron," Marcus said sharply, "Didn't I tell you to carry the trays? They are too bulky for Samantha."

Mini Marcus looked up at his father,

"Yes, sir. Sorry Sam," Aaron said, taking the tray out of the kitchen and in the direction of the library.

Samantha was leaning against the counter, her hand protectively resting on her swollen stomach, her face pale.

"You look tired," Marcus said, putting his arm around Samantha's shoulder. "Why don't you go upstairs. We can handle this. You've had a long enough day."

Samantha smiled weakly and took off her apron, hanging it on the hook by the door.

"Thank you. See you in the morning," she said, disappearing into the hallway.

Beth continued to watch as Samantha slowly made her way up the stairs.

Beth turned back to Marcus who now had the water pitchers filled with ice and water and was wiping the outsides dry. She quickly realized this was the first time she and Marcus had been alone together since the rain last night. Beth felt suddenly uncomfortable.

"What exactly is this tonight?" Beth asked, hiding her feelings.

Before Marcus could answer, Aaron and the black-haired girl had come back into the kitchen.

"Beth, this is Abby," Marcus said, indicating the girl, "And this is my son Aaron. This is Beth, the woman I told you about."

"The one with the old Bug?" Abby asked with a smile, "I love your car."

"Thank you, Abby," Beth said, matching the girl's smile. "When I get her back, I'll give you a ride."

"Come on Abby," Aaron said, picking up another tray. Abby smiled again and took the water pitchers from Marcus and followed a frowning Aaron down the hall.

Beth heard a loud pounding coming from what she guessed was the library.

"Sounds like the meeting is about to start," Marcus said. "Come join us."

CHAPTER 13

Fred Wickman, owner of the Wickman House Inn and honorary chair of the Door County Preservation Society, banged his gavel on the podium set up next to the table of food. At 5 foot seven and sporting a shock white beard, mustache, and wavy hair, Fred looked like a friendly Santa Claus. What made him look even more convincing as Santa was a belly which appeared to have indulged on too many of Edna Anderson's pastries and ice cream sundaes from Wilson's.

"Please everyone," Fred said, banging his gavel again, "Please find a seat, and we can get down to the reason you are all here tonight."

Marcus and Beth found a seat on the sofa near the fireplace. Across the room, Beth could see Deputy Neuville, tonight wearing jeans and a Packers jersey, standing behind the chair Abby was seated in. Deputy Neuville smiled and nodded in Beth's direction. Aaron came over and sat on the floor next to the sofa.

When the room quieted down and most everyone was seated, Fred began speaking again.

"First off, I would like to thank all of you for coming out tonight. I know how hard that can be for some of you with Maifest next weekend and the beginning of our season. I will try to keep this short, which is not always my strong suit."

Knowing laughter was the reply to that comment.

"I would like everyone to say thank you to Edna tonight for allowing us to gather here and for working so hard on this wonderful array of food."

Whistles and applause followed. Edna beamed with a mix of joy and embarrassment.

"Now, to get down to the real reason for this meeting. As many of you know, Ruth Dickerson, owner of the Sunset Bar and Grill, was taken to Sturgeon Bay last week and is now in hospice care.

Since there are no living relatives, Miss Dickerson's estate has been put into the care of the Hanson Krueger law office. As per her request, the property will be put up for sale."

This proclamation was met with disappointed and surprised moans, 'no's', and 'what's'.

"Please quiet down," Fred said over the group.

"I know this is quite a shock."

"The Sunset has been part of the peninsula for over 100 years," someone in the crowd said.

"I know how important the restaurant is," Fred continued "We all have…"

Fred's sentence was drowned out by overlapping voices from the crowd.

"I learned to cook there," a voice in the crowd said.

"It was my first job," someone else said.

"They can't sell it," came a third voice.

"Quiet please," Fred said, banging his gavel until the crowd had mostly settled down. "I know how important the Sunset is to many of us," Fred repeated. "But unfortunately, there are no heirs, and the property will be sold. James Krueger gave me the heads up as a courtesy to the Society. This information won't be publicly released for a while, at least not until the assessors come and determine a price."

"Then some out of towners can swoop in and tear the Sunset down and put up condos for tourists," the first commenter said.

"There will have to be a hearing on property use first," Fred said over more murmuring from the group. "I know we all don't want more development of the waterfront areas, which is why James talked with me. I am hoping if we put some thought into what you heard here tonight, the Preservation Society can come up with ways to raise the funds to buy the property ourselves."

"What about grants or business development monies? Or…"

The voices of the crowd continued with questions as Aaron tapped against his father's leg.

"What is he doing here?" Aaron asked Marcus.

Marcus looked in the direction Aaron was indicating.

Leaning against the wall was a man in his thirties. Unlike most of the group, he was not dressed casually but rather in a dark grey suit and dress shoes. He was intently listening to the crowd's questions, all the while flicking a gold cigarette lighter open and shut.

Beth noticed the unhappy look on Marcus's face.

"Who is that?" Beth asked,

"That's Carlson Ross," Marcus replied with a huff. "As in Ross Construction and Ross Enterprises and Ross Management group. It seems the Preservation Society may not be the only group to be told of the potential sale of property."

"Is that bad?" Beth asked, genuinely not understanding.

"Did you see the big stone and glass building just north of Sturgeon Bay when you drove through? Or the monster of the hotel blocking the water view coming into Ephraim," Aaron said.

"Honestly, no," Beth replied, "It was raining."

"Figures," Aaron said, standing up and walking across the room.

"Aaron!" Marcus said angrily, not that Aaron could hear him.

"You have to forgive my son," Marcus said, turning to Beth. "He's angry, not that I blame him. The Ross Group came here about ten years ago and began buying up empty properties. They proceeded to build whatever they wanted on the land. If a village or township wouldn't grant them permission, they would buy land somewhere else, allowing the original property to become an eyesore, and build where there were no regulations. They destroyed a lot of hunting lands, and people are not happy with them."

"And you are afraid they will do the same to the Sunset property?" Beth asked.

"I don't really expect you to fully understand how important that land and business is to a great many of us, but yes. I don't just think they will tear down the Sunset and build condos, I know they will. They have been pressuring Ruth for the past ten years to sell. Unfortunately, buying that property will take a lot more than a few bake sales and donations to accomplish."

Beth noticed that many of the people in attendance had filtered out of the room, not waiting for the official end of the meeting to be announced. Judging by the sideways glances and out right stares being given to Carlson Ross, Beth assumed the others in the meeting shared Marcus's feelings about Ross and his companies.

CHAPTER 14

Edna didn't say much while she packed away the leftover baked goods in the kitchen. Beth noticed she didn't have her usual smile either. With the Marshalls and Beth the only guests for the night, there wasn't much to prepare for morning breakfast besides the egg bake and sausage to go along with the muffins.

"Are you sure you don't want me to help you clean up?" Beth asked, breaking the silence.

"Yes, my dear," Edna replied, "Everything has been cleared from the library, and I sent everyone else home already. Abby and Aaron have school in the morning, and Chad is working tonight."

"Chad?"

"You met him the other night, but he was in uniform then,"

"Oh, Deputy Neuville," Beth said, putting the pieces together. "So that is Abby's dad."

"Yes. I let Abby work here on the weekends so her father can get some sleep after he gets home. Laura, Abby's mother, works days at the hospital in the city so I like to help them out while I can."

"Can I ask you a question?" Beth said, pulling a chair out from under the table and sitting down.

"Of course you can," Edna replied, sitting down on her own chair.

"Marcus said something before he left tonight, he said 'I don't really expect you to fully understand how important that land and business is to a great many of us.' What do you think he meant by that?"

"Here in the county, we are rich in history. There are traditions many of us treasure, and places. One of those places is the Sunset Bar and Grill. When the Dickerson family moved here in 1850, lumber mills and the stone quarry were big business. The first house had been built in Sturgeon Bay and other communities were coming together as well. Southern Door was already occupied with Belgian and German immigrants, and Scandinavian and Icelandic immigrants were venturing north. There were Potawatomi Indians living here as well. All these groups formed communities and brought their traditions with them.

Seeing a need for worker housing and inexpensive food, Elroy Dickerson built the original Sunset. It was originally called The Resting Sun. The bar was on the first floor, and the rental rooms were on the upper level. Elroy and his wife Minnie kept the workers warm and well fed. When money was tight, they took in fresh vegetables and eggs and game meat in exchange for rent. They always felt it was better to share what you had whenever you could and that the good deeds would come back to you.

"When the great fire came in October of 1871..."

"The Chicago Fire?" Beth interrupted.

"No, the Peshtigo Fire," Edna replied as she rose to get a pair of pie slices and two glasses of milk from the refrigerator. Setting them down on the table, Edna continued. "Peshtigo is located across the bay, and the fire started the same day as the Chicago fire but did much more damage. Some of the fires even reached into the lower part of the county here and stopped short of Sawyer, or what is now the west side of Sturgeon Bay. When Minnie found out about the fires, she and her sister Belle took all the extra blankets and pillows to those who lost their homes and were sheltered at the churches that still stood in Southern Door. Unoccupied rooms at the tavern were given to the displaced people for free or in exchange for work. That act of kindness solidified the Dickerson's as a staple of the community."

"In 1900," Edna continued, "the tavern was expanded. A second wing was built, and a bakery and cooking school started. The workings of the tavern and restaurant were now taken over by the younger generation, who moved into the tavern, and it was renamed The Sunset."

"When more and more people began to come to the towns and villages of the county just to visit, more and more businesses were established. Restaurants and bars and hotels popped up. Many of the cooks and bartenders came to the Sunset to learn how to prepare meals. Nearly everyone had worked at the Sunset at one time or another, me included. Because of that family, The Sunset Bar and Grill, as it became known, was the place to visit and work at. The restaurant became as much of a member of the peninsula as the people themselves."

"And to see it torn down and built over with million-dollar summer homes or condos." Beth commented, "would be like one of the founding families dying."

"Yes, exactly," Edna replied. "I am glad you can appreciate that idea. Now, we need to get to bed and think of how to help preserve a treasure from vanishing."

CHAPTER 15

It was 9:45 when Beth went up to her room. As she went past Samantha's room, she could hear soft moans. Beth paused for a few minutes unsure if she should knock to check on Samantha or not. When rhythmic snores replaced the moans, Beth continued down the hall to her room.

As Beth changed into her pajamas, she thought about the meeting and the story Edna had told her. In Boulder there was always some older building being razed and a new one being built. Subdivisions and more hotels than she could count were constantly under construction. Reporting on all the parties and groundbreakings had kept her busy. Thankfully, the job allowed her to work in her office at home, something Terry had insisted on if she had to work.

What had Annie said? Party planning and organizing? Perhaps there was something she could offer to help with. But first she had to find a place to live.

Beth stretched and sat down in the rocking chair. The table next to the rocker held several books, all with a white sticker proclaiming, 'local author'. She picked each book up and read the descriptions on the back of each of them. As she went to the stack. she came across the one Emily had been reading that morning, Juniper's Dragon by Thomas Davis. Not only did the book have a local author sticker but also a gold Signed Copy sticker. Beth sat the book down on the table as a to-be read-book and chose instead a murder mystery set in New Orleans and started reading.

Beth was startled awake by loud voices and movement in the hall outside. Getting out of the rocker, she glanced at the clock which read 11:13. She noted the book she had been reading was now on the floor.

The loud voices continued in the hall, joined now by Edna's sounding frantic and concerned. Beth noticed red flashing lights reflecting in the mirror coming from the parking lot below her window. When she opened her door, she could see Samantha's door was also open. Deputy Neuville was giving Edna a hug and telling her everything was going to be alright. Marcus was holding Edna's hand.

Noticing Beth's door had opened; Marcus kissed Edna on the cheek and went over to Beth.

"Samantha's water broke. The paramedics say her contractions are still light, but they're not taking any chances. Her blood pressure is high, and they don't like that. I already called her mom and her brother. They should both be at the hospital by morning."

"She was so pale earlier, I thought something looked wrong," Beth said, concern in her voice.

"They will take good care of her at the hospital," Deputy Neuville said as he walked Edna towards Beth's door. "My wife had our four kids there, so I should know. It's nice to meet you again and under better circumstances."

"You too," Beth replied. Not knowing what else to say.

"Please let me know if you hear anything, Miss Edna," Chad said, "Marcus, can you pick up Abby after school tomorrow? She only has a half day, and I have a training in the afternoon."

"Anything for my goddaughter," Marcus said.

"And I can use the help tomorrow if you don't mind," Edna added.

"She likes helping you out," Chad replied, "And I know she would love to play the new piano piece she is learning. I have to get back to work. I hope this is my only call tonight, I need the quiet before the weekend when the population blows up."

"Have a good night," Edna said. "There is still rice pie in the kitchen."

The three stood in the hall until Chad disappeared around the curve of the staircase.

"Well, that was a little excitement for the night," Marcus said as Beth opened the door to her room. "Cute pajamas."

Beth looked down at her outfit and was horrified when she realized she had changed into her blue and silver pajamas with silver stars. But in her defense, she had planned to relax for the night.

Noting the suitcases were still where she had placed them in the morning, Edna went into Beth's room.

"You haven't unpacked?" she asked.

"I didn't know how long I could afford to stay here so I left everything packed," Beth replied. "I had planned on looking around for work tomorrow and a place to rent."

"Don't worry about that my dear," Edna said with a light chuckle.

"What?" Beth asked, confused.

"I think what Edna is trying not to say," Marcus added, "Is that a room and job has just opened. Isn't that right, Edna?"

"That is, if you want it, dear," Edna said.

"Really?" Beth asked, still trying to comprehend what was happening. "I mean yes. If you want me."

"We can work out the details in the morning," Edna said. "I think we have had enough excitement for one night."

Beth watched Edna and Marcus start walking down the hall and down the steps. Beth heard a gentle meow coming from inside her room.

"You cannot sleep in my room all night," Beth told Cleo as she picked him up from the bed. "What do you think? Should I take your mama up on the offer and work here for a while?"

Cleo let out a soft meow and butted Beth on the arm as Beth gently set the cat on the floor in the hall and shut the door. Beth could hear another meow from the other side of the door.

When Beth woke up the next morning, she showered, dressed, and opened the door, ready to start her new job.

Cleo was curled up outside the door. He looked up at Beth with sleepy eyes, stood up and followed Beth downstairs to the kitchen.

CHAPTER 16

"Is summer always this busy?" Beth asked Edna while continuing to rub her bare feet,

"I swear I put on 15 miles of walking today."

"This is just the first weekend of summer my dear," Edna replied, bringing out a tray and setting it on the table next to Beth. "Maifest is always the official start of the tourist season. And with 2024 being the 50th anniversary of the event, this year was extra special, and extra busy."

"I was told the highway 57 side of the county was the quiet side."

"Just wait until the 4th of July weekend," Edna said, handing Beth a glass of iced tea. "Kringle?"

"I ate so much today I am not sure I could have another bite."

Settling into the other porch chair, Edna took a swallow of her tea. "I see you are on babysitting duty tonight," she said.

"Olive has been fed, changed, and is now sleeping," replied Beth. "That is until I stop rocking."

"Rose loved being rocked out here too. We would sit here once all the guests were taken care of and just rock and listen to nature. Rose would laugh at the squirrels. Earl told Rose, if she sat real still, perhaps a very brave squirrel would come and eat a peanut out of her hand."

"And did it work?"

"Once in a while, but it kept Rose quiet just in case."

Both women sat silent for a few minutes, the only movement was rocking Olive and drinking tea.

"Rose is your daughter?" Beth asked, breaking the silence.

"Was my daughter," Edna replied, her voice slow and unsteady. "Our Rose died just shy of her 12th birthday. She would be turning 41 this August."

"What hap…" Beth started to ask, however Edna continued,

"Rose was born with a heart murmur. The doctors discovered it shortly after she was born. We tried so hard to keep her life as normal and quiet as possible. We lived up the road aways, and whenever I took Rose out for a walk in her buggy, I would tell her how much I loved this house. Somehow Earl found out, and for our anniversary that year, he came home with the deed, the keys, and the crazy notion to open a Bed and Breakfast. It took a full year to put everything together from decor to menu. But we did it. Over the next few years, we worked on the gardens and the patio and the gazebos. Rose would follow me to the gardens once she learned to walk. I think her first words, besides mama and papa, were names of the flowers, and that included her name."

Edna stopped long enough to pour another glass of tea for the two of them before continuing.

"One day we were out pulling weeds, and Rose just stopped. She stopped moving, stopped talking, and by the time the ambulance arrived, stopped breathing. Her heart gave out.

That was when we changed the name from Inn of the Pines to The Rose Garden Inn."

"And decorated the rooms in floral themes?" Beth asked.

"Doing that made it feel as though Rose was still here," Edna said, wiping a tear from her eye. "You have the Rose Room. I keep that one open for emergencies. Then there is Orchid, Sunflower, Daisy, Clover, Marigold, Tulip, Aster, Foxglove, Lily of the Valley, and of course Trillium rooms."

"I think Rose is here with you," Beth said softly. "And I know she would love every room in this place just as much as she loved the gardens."

The buzzer in the kitchen went off, indicating someone had pressed the bell at the front desk and startled Olive who began to cry. Beth picked her up and held her, patted her back and started to softly sing a lullaby. Edna went into the kitchen, leaving Beth and Olive alone on the porch.

A few minutes later Beth heard the screen door open.

"Edna said I would find you out here," Marcus said, walking onto the back porch.

"Shh," Beth replied softly. "I finally got her to sleep,"

Only then did Marcus see the sleeping baby snuggled in Beth's lap.

"Who is this little angel?" Marcus asked, putting his hand on the baby's curly brown hair.

"This is Olive, the Richardson's baby from the Aster room upstairs. They wanted to catch the movies at the Skyway, and I said I would watch her for the night."

"You seem to be a natural holding a baby," Marcus said, settling himself in the chair next to Beth and Olive. "I can't believe you never had children of your own."

With Marcus's comment, Beth stopped rocking, a faraway look washing over her face.

Her words came out slowly. "That was not my choice. Terry always said after."

"After what?"

"Everything," Beth replied. "After he graduated college. After we got married. After he landed a job at a firm. After we bought a house. After. After. After. Well, after never came. What did come was 'too late'."

Olive cooed and fussed in Beth's lap.

"Shh," Beth whispered and began rocking again. Olive responded with more coos and wiggles before falling to sleep once more, thumb in her mouth.

Marcus and Beth sat in silence, neither one knowing what to say next. The only sounds were the scraping of wood on wood from Beth's rocking chair, the occasional whoosh of a car passing in front of the inn, and dozens of overlapping high pitched chirps coming from the fields behind the inn.

"What is that?" Beth asked.

"Spring Peepers," Marcus answered. "The swamp is full of them. When I was a kid, my dog Sheppy would hear the little frogs and try to catch them. We always knew how deep the swamp was by how wet that dog was. Mom made me give him a bath before allowing the dog into the house after his hunt."

"Did he ever catch them?"

"Nope. But that never stopped him from trying. Sheppy was a good dog."

"Have you thought about getting another dog?"

"Thought about it. But I had my own set of afters. After a steady job. After the wedding. After Aaron got older. Then Sarah got sick, and the idea of caring for another living creature just didn't fit."

"There's no ticking clock on pets like there is on babies."

"I went down to Sturgeon a few times to check out the humane society. Just never was brave enough to go in. Besides, coming here and visiting Cleo is my animal therapy."

On cue, the large grey cat appeared from under the porch. With a rather loud meow, Cleo bumped up against Marcus' leg before jumping into his lap. Marcus lifted his hand to allow Cleo more room. Cleo's purrs joined in harmony with the peepers, accented by tiny soft snores from Olive.

Beth closed her eyes, taking in the night sounds.

"It must be nice living here. Everything is so quiet and dark at night. I cannot believe how many stars I have been able to see out my window."

"The farther you get from the lights of the city, the less distraction there is, and the more you can see. If you are here in August, we can go up to Newport State Park and see the meteor shower. Did you know that Newport State Park is the only International Dark Sky Park in Wisconsin?"

"I did not know," Beth replied.

"Well, now you do," Marcus said, a self-satisfied smile on his face.

Olive began to fuss and wake up. The gentle fussing quickly turned into a cry.

"Sounds like someone is hungry," Marcus said. He stood up and opened the screen door for Beth, "Anything I can do to help?"

"There is a bottle in the refrigerator," Beth replied, gently patting Olive on the back to soothe her crying.

Marcus was already halfway to the kitchen before Beth had finished what she was saying.

Beth settled into the highbacked chair in the lounge area by the bay window. She turned down the light on the side table and stared out the window searching the night sky for stars, still patting Olive on the back.

"I think I could get used to this place," she said to herself.

CHAPTER 17

"Lord love a duck."

Beth stopped short outside the library doors where the outburst had come from. When something soft hit the door, she cautiously opened it, not wanting to be target to whatever was coming next.

Marcus was seated at the paper filled desk, and he didn't look happy. Paper wads sat strewn around the room.

"Is everything alright?" Beth asked.

"No, everything is not alright," Marcus snapped. "I am looking into grant proposals or at least trying to."

Beth took in a quick, deep breath at Marcus' outburst. "I'm sorry," she said, her voice shaking. "I can leave you alone."

Marcus looked up from the desk and paperwork and saw the pained, and maybe a bit scared, expression on Beth's face.

"Don't leave," Marcus said, his tone low and steady, "I'm sorry I yelled. These forms are just so…"

"Annoying? Frustrating? Confusing?"

"All of the above. It's like they are asking the same question five times over, expecting a different answer. Like they want to trip you up or something."

"They are government forms. What do you expect?" Beth said, walking towards the desk. "Almost as bad as life insurance policies."

"Or hospital bills."

"Let me look," Beth said, kneeling next to the desk and taking the top paper Marcus had just put down. She stared at it for a minute, took another paper and compared it to the first.

"Here's your problem," Beth said, setting both sets of papers on the desk.

"This one here," she continued. "Is 1700LC. It is used for purchasing land only, no buildings." She set the stack of papers on the floor. "Now this one is 1700LCO. This allows land purchases with outbuildings that can be torn down if they're no more than 7600 square feet total."

"If you say so," Marcus said with a slight laugh. "How do you know this?"

"Terry is a lawyer. Case notes and legal briefs were considered pillow talk," Beth replied with a shrug.

"Oh, Ok," was the only answer Marcus could think of.

In the past three weeks, Beth had only mentioned Terry and her life in Colorado only twice, and both were in anger. Marcus felt he knew more about Beth's friend Annie and her kids than he did about Beth herself.

"Please move," Beth said, interrupting Marcus' thoughts. Beth stood up and started to gently push Marcus off the desk chair."

"Of course."

"This form is for a building only, no property." Beth tossed those forms to the floor with the others. "Do you not have a secretary position assigned to your Preservation Society?"

"We have a position, just no one filling it right now," Marcus admitted, feeling more than a little sheepish, "Amber Lottes was our secretary, but she got married last December and moved to Milwaukee."

"Well, that was bad timing," Beth said, "And you haven't replaced her yet?"

"No," Marcus answered, looking even more sheepish than before.

Beth sighed and shook her head as she pulled and tossed more papers.

"Here it is," Beth said, as she held a form up for Marcus to see.

"You could always fill the role," Marcus said with a grin.

"How do you know I will be staying very long?"

"Where would you go? Considering I still have the keys for Betty."

"You do," Beth exclaimed and stared wide mouthed at Marcus, who was grinning ear to ear.

"If I am going to help you, and get Betty back, I am going to need iced tea, and lots of it."

"If you can figure out this bureaucratic mess, you can have anything you want," Marcus said as he walked out the door.

"How about some Belgian Pie?"

"Coming up."

"Raisin. With a glass of milk."

"Whatever you want dear."

"You are a 501C-3? Correct?" Beth called out after Marcus' retreating form.

Marcus wondered where the 'dear' comment came from. All he could hope for right now was that Beth hadn't heard it or was too intent on the task at hand to have noticed.

CHAPTER 18

Beth sat at the picnic table in the back yard of the Inn. Two handcrafted pottery bowls sat on the table in front of her. With the sun going down, she had tossed a sweater over her shoulders but was still wearing the denim shorts she had worn all day at the festival. Her cellphone was tucked between her shoulder and chin.

"So, you're gonna tell me you spent a whole day selling corn dogs and keychains while people watched a flock of goats climb a ladder to sit on a roof?" Annie's laugh erupted from the other end of Beth's cell phone.

"Yes, I did," Beth replied, tossing another freshly hulled strawberry into one of the bowls.

"And it is a herd of goats, not a flock, and they walk up a ramp not a ladder."

"So, people come out and watch this? All day?"

"Not all day. Just during the roofing of the goats-parade."

"A whole parade? Of goats?"

"People walk the parade too. And they can bring their pets with them."

"If you're gonna tell me they dress in goat costumes, I'm hanging up."

"Sarcasm noted," Beth said with a chuckle, "And it is the pets, not the people who dress in goat costumes. Though there were a few colorful individuals, I must admit."

"And this is Northeastern Wisconsin fun?"

"You are a fine one to talk, coming from a town where the highlight of the year is a celebration of Frozen Dead Guy Day."

"Don't diss the old guy in the tuff shed!" Annie said with a laugh, "You had fun with the coffin races, too."

"And the Dead Man Ice Cream," Beth replied, matching Annie's laugh. "I imagine every small town has their own quirky events."

Beth straightened her stiff shoulders, and the phone fell into the ever-growing pile of strawberry hulls.

"Sorry, Annie," she said raising her voice, "I dropped you.'"

"I didn't feel a thing," Annie replied, still laughing. "What are you doing?"

"Hulling strawberries," Beth said, picking the leaves off her phone and raising it to her ear, setting the metal huller on the table. "Edna is showing me how to make fresh shortcakes in the morning for the guests."

"Now that is somethin' I would pay to see. Miss, 'my produce comes from their natural habitat of the grocery store'."

"I picked the berries myself from the greenhouse this morning."

"Before the goat march," Annie laughed again.

"Goat parade." Beth corrected, "And believe it or not, picking strawberries is very relaxing. Next week I will be learning how to make homemade chicken pot pie."

"And I suppose you're gonna tell me you'll be pluckin' the feathers yourself."

"No, I will be going to the Main Street Market for those. There are grocery stores up here."

There was a pause in the conversation as Beth stood up and shook off the hulls and stems from her apron and put them in the brown bag for the compost heap.

Somewhere in the distance a robin chirped followed by another, returning the song. Beth took in a deep breath.

"You really are enjoyin' your adventure, aren't ya?" Annie said, bringing Beth back to reality.

"I am," Beth replied, "I can do what I want when I am done working. I can dress in shorts and tank tops if I want. Eat when and what I want. And I have money to spend on myself. Tomorrow, I have off, and Terry is taking ..." Beth stopped, realizing her mistake. "I mean, Marcus is going to... Oh, crap."

"You, Ok?" Annie asked after a brief, uncomfortable silence. "Beth?"

"I am not sure why I said that," Beth said, fighting back the tears threatening to escape.

"It is so stupid. I have been…"

Beth stopped talking, not sure what to say next. She reached up to the chain around her neck and touched the rings hanging there.

"Thirty years with one guy is hard to let go of, even if he is a world class jerk," Annie said, trying to sound sympathetic. "Have you talked to Terry since you left?"

"Once," Beth admitted, "He asked when I was going to grow up and come back home to him. Any other time I hung up before the end of the answering machine message. What about you, have you seen him?

"He tracked me down at home that Sunday you left. I told him you were pissed after he ditched you on your anniversary. He thought ya can't be mad at him for workin'."

"And what did he have to say to that?"

"He thinks you're gonna come back as soon as ya calm down and realize ya made a mistake."

"Sounds about right," Beth said with a sigh.

"A couple days later he came to the salon. Said he was gonna call the cops and that I was hidin' you."

"You told him no, right?"

"Of course I did, hon," Annie replied, "I would never give you up to that narcissistic, self-centered, self-absorbed, son of a..." Annie stopped before finishing that thought.

"Tell me what you really feel," Beth said, trying her best to smile but failing.

"I have to go now," Beth continued, all previous happiness gone from her voice. "Five in the morning comes way too early."

"You'll call me tomorrow night?" Annie asked, noting Beth's tone.

"I'll call you tomorrow."

"Long distance pinkie swear?"

"Long distance pinkie swear."

The phone clicked off. Beth reached again for the wedding rings, then tucked them into her top with a sigh, something that was becoming more and more frequent.

Talking with Annie had been a bit of a distraction from the events of the day, but the stares, and sideways glances she and Marcus had been given during the parade and especially after while they were at the restaurant, still bothered her. The whispered conversations echoed back to her early days whenever there was a party or award banquet at Terry's firm. Terry, still a junior partner, would parade her out in front of his colleagues. She was always made to "dress to impress" as Terry would say, usually, always, in what he wanted her to wear. The next day the borrowed jewelry would go back to the stores, and Terry would go back to work, pleased to have made a good impression. Why she thought being here where no one knew her should be any different was beyond her thought process. Absently she took another few strawberries and popped them in her mouth, not really tasting them. She closed her eyes and sighed again.

"Penny for your thoughts?"

Beth sat up straight. She hadn't heard the squeak of the screen door or Edna coming towards her.

"I didn't mean to startle you, my dear," Edna said, placing another bowl of unhulled strawberries on the table. "It looks to me like your thoughts are worth a great deal more than a penny tonight. Did you have another bad phone call with your ex?"

Beth did not bother even trying to correct Edna that Terry and she were still married. It wasn't worth the effort. Besides, the word ex was starting to sound comforting coming from Edna.

"No, I was talking to my best friend, Annie," Beth replied, "I was telling her about the goats."

"That shouldn't have been a cause for the deep sighs."

"It's not. I was just..." Beth stopped not really knowing how to finish that sentence.

"Well, my Earl always said, hulling strawberries and shucking corn could solve all the world's problems. There just isn't enough shucking and hulling going on today."

"Maybe that should be a new law," Beth said, forcing a small smile.

"I think I will bring that up at the next council meeting." Edna replied, matching Beth's smile.

Both reached for a strawberry in the bowl and began to take the bright green stems off. Cleo, having followed Edna to the table, jumped onto the table and began playing with the strawberry stems.

Beth tossed her stem in the cat's direction and Cleo caught it, tucked it under his grey belly, and lay down on it. Neither of the women said a word. The only sounds were the click of the metal strawberry hullers and loud purrs from Cleo.

"I saw the way Mrs. Thompson and Mrs. Wilson were looking at you and Marcus holding hands during the parade," Edna said, breaking the silence.

Beth sighed once again.

"Don't let it get to you, dear," Edna continued. "They are two of the busiest busy bodies in all of Sister Bay, maybe even the whole county. When my family moved her in 1968, and they found out my parents weren't married, they almost threw us out of the church," Edna continued talking as the strawberry bowl continued filling. "Then, when I married Earl only four short years after his Katherine died, I thought they were going to run us out of the county. Earl had a plan to get back at them though."

"This I have to hear," Beth said, eating yet another berry.

"You have to understand that both Mrs. Wilson and Mrs. Thompson's husbands had died in an ice fishing accident."

"Is that what made them so nosey?" Beth asked.

"It wasn't the fact the men died so tragically, but rather the embarrassment of knowing their husbands met their end in an incident involving muskets from the civil war reenactments, a bad map of where the best pike were, too little of ice, and way too much Pabst Blue Ribbon."

"Oh," was all Beth could say, looking up with a quizzical look and a strawberry in her hand.

"But that is not the story I was telling you," Edna continued, "When those two busybodies tried to get Earl to quit the Peninsula singers because of me, he and Fred Wickman hotwired Mr. Lewis's BMW, Mr. Lewis, being 31 and the new and very handsome single science teacher at Gibraltar High School and parked it in front of Wilson/Thompson duplex overnight on Easter weekend. Talk about stares and whispers."

"Your husband sounds like quite a character," Beth said with a laugh.

"He was. 32 years together was not enough," Edna replied. "But we built this place with his love of people and my baking. Even though I wasn't a native, and he was 6th generation, he never made me feel unwanted. And he never let anyone in town treat me that way either."

"I think I would have liked your Earl."

"I know he would have liked you, my dear," Edna said, sweeping up the strawberry hulls that hadn't made it into the garbage bowl. "Now, let me tell you what I think has made you sigh, and you feel free to correct me if I am wrong or get too personal. There are a few things I have learned in my 73 years. First, you can live in Door County for 40 years and still not be a 'local'.

"Second, church and social events are, more often than not, scheduled around Packer games.

"Finally, people who come to a strange place on a whim are either looking for something or running from something."

Edna picked up the bowl with the strawberry stems and indicated for Beth to take the other. She then turned towards the porch and stopped, Cleo at her heels. "So, my dear, do you care to tell me which one it is?"

Beth picked up the berry bowl and stood up. Another sigh.

Not turning around to look at Edna, "Can it be both?" Beth asked.

CHAPTER 19

"Don't let him bother you so much," Edna said softly, noticing Beth glancing in the direction of the kitchen table. Since the two of them had started to wash the dishes and Abby and Aaron were peeling cucumbers and slicing tomatoes, many such looks had been exchanged.

The bell at the front desk rang loudly,

"I'll get it," Abby said, already standing up and removing her apron.

Aaron stood and followed Abby from the room but not without giving another look toward the sink.

"What is it with him?" Beth asked as the door swung closed behind the couple, "Ever since Saturday he's looked at me like I just killed his favorite pet."

"He's a feisty one," Edna said, shaking the water off the plate she was drying. "Takes after his mother, that's for sure. I think Aaron has been noticing how much time Marcus has been spending over here and not just tilling the gardens and painting the porch."

"I am not following," Beth replied.

"Aaron's mother Sarah died two years ago this March," Edna explained, "Complications from diabetes. She kept everything to herself. Once she had to start dialysis, Marcus quit his job at the shipyard and stayed home caring for her. Now, if Marcus even talks to a woman, Aaron gets upset. He tries anything he can to chase them off. Dirty shame too, Marcus is still so young."

"Being a teen is not easy, especially when it comes to losing a parent."

"Sounds as though you talk from experience. When did you lose someone?"

"Mom, when I was eight," Beth said, "My father drank himself to death when I was 19. Annie said it was a combination of loneliness and cheap whiskey."

Beth had never shared that bit of her history with anyone except Annie, but there was something about the older woman's candor and smiling blue eyes that made Beth feel she could trust her with anything.

"Now that you know a bit more about Marcus and Aaron, come sit, and you can answer my question from the other night."

"Excuse me?"

"Are you running from or running to?" Edna said, pulling out a chair at the table and holding a metal peeler and cucumber out in Beth's direction.

Beth poured herself a tall glass of iced tea and sighed. Perhaps it was time to tear off the bandage, and Edna was easy to talk to. In fact, she reminded Beth a great deal of her grandmother in many ways.

"I suppose it is a bit of both," Beth said, taking the peeler and sitting in the chair opposite Edna.

"Bad relationship," Edna said, phrasing her words in more of a statement rather than a question.

"How did you know?"

"I may be old, but I am not blind," Edna replied. "Your ring, or should I say the finger where your ring used to be. I can see the tan lines have not faded, so it must have been a recent break up."

"More of a leaving really," Beth said, reaching up and feeling for the chain around her neck.

"And you can't quite find the words or the heart to call it quits."

"I met Terry right after my father died when I was in my first year of college. By junior year, we were married in a tiny civil ceremony. Everything was fresh and new and happy. We moved into Terry's apartment in Boulder, and everything started to change. We could only afford for one of us to finish school, so, being very traditional, we decided Terry should finish. He said when he graduated it would be my turn. But my turn never seemed to happen. With each new 'advancement,' as Terry put it, things became more about him and his career. I tried to be patient, but I was not satisfied. My car was not good enough, or my clothes, or my job. I just was not happy."

"Did you try talking to him?"

"We talked. We fought. We made up. Things would be better for a while, and then Terry would fall into the same patterns, and eventually he would start bringing his work home with him, and things would fall apart again."

"Sounds to me like a very one-sided relationship."

"Relationship?" Beth said with a sigh. "There was no relationship. We slept in the same bed, and that was it. In public, Terry made it look as though we had the perfect marriage, so much so that I almost believed it was. But the truth was, our marriage was held together with duct tape and birthday wishes."

"So, what brought you here?"

"For our silver wedding anniversary, my husband decided he would pull an all-night work session with a client. So, I took my car, the credit card and savings, and drove. I remembered coming here as a child before mom died. Then my car stalled in the pouring rain, and I ended up in a strange man's front yard. The End."

Beth took in a deep breath and sighed before taking a drink of her tea, her hands shaking.

"The Good Lord tends to put us all in a certain place at a certain time," Edna said, placing her hands on Beth's and helped Beth lower the glass to the table. "We may not always know His plans, but we find out soon enough."

Beth looked up from her glass and matched Edna's smile with one of her own.

Both women looked down at Edna's full bowl of peeled cucumbers and Beth's nearly empty one.

"You don't peel many cucumbers, do you?" Edna asked, her smile widening.

Beth shook her head,

"I have to admit, most of my meals came pre-made from the deli and frozen foods section."

'We will have to change that," Edna said, peeler in one hand and cucumber in the other, "Here, let me show you."

Just then, the kitchen door opened, and Aaron stuck his head inside.

"Dad called," he said with a scowl. "He wants you to come out tonight after the baseball game and meet some more friends. He asked me to drive you."

As quickly as he had come in, Aaron disappeared out the door again.

"That boy needs to be reined in a bit," Edna said, picking up the cucumber bowls and carrying them to the counter.

"No," Beth replied, "He needs to let go a little."

CHAPTER 20

The trip from the inn to Sister Bay Bowl was only ten minutes, but the tension in the cab of Marcus's car made it seem much longer.

"So, what grade will you be going into this fall?" Beth asked, trying to break through the silence.

"Senior," was Aaron's answer.

"Are you planning on college after that?"

"Maybe."

"Your father told me you are starting work at Pirate's Cove Monday," Beth said, hoping a change in subject might lead to a conversation.

"Yep," another one-word answer.

Beth sighed and leaned back against the leather headrest.

"We're here," Aaron said, pulling into a parking spot.

At least Aaron can say more than one word, Beth thought to herself.

Aaron was out of the truck and heading over to join Wade Kole, Kenny Johnson and Andy Kress sitting on the front porch of the Bowl. Andy and Wade quickly crushed out their cigarettes when Beth approached and turned away. Abby was perched on the white metal railing along with another girl, Angel Rose. Both had their cell phones out and were showing them to each other, excitingly talking about something on the phones.

"Hi Beth," Abby said, looking up just long enough to acknowledge Beth walking up the steps before looking down at her phone. Beth returned the greeting, not sure whether Abby heard it.

The front door was open, and as she walked closer, Beth was hit by the strong smell of fried chicken and beer. She took a deep breath in, enjoying the spicy scent.

"Beth, over here," called Marcus from his seat at the bar. "I saved you a seat," he continued, patting a brown leather barstool between himself and Chad Neuville.

Beth smiled at the men, happy to see familiar faces among the dozen or more occupants who had turned her way when Marcus had called out to her. Beth suddenly felt uncomfortable with so many eyes on her. Chad took her hand and helped her up onto the bar stool.

"Thank you, Deputy," Beth said, accepting the hand up.

"No need to be formal," Chad said, "I'm off duty. Just call me Chad."

There was a gentleness in Chad's tone which made Beth feel comfortable despite the fact he was over a foot taller and about 100 pounds heavier. Between Chad and Marcus, Beth felt dwarfed but also able to hide from all the unfamiliar stares.

Both men were absorbed in conversation which gave Beth a chance to take in the room. Most of the room was warm, polished wood. Black and white photographs hung on the walls showing what Beth could only assume to be the history of this bar and bowling alley.

The floor was large black and ivory squares, again adding to the old fashion charm of the restaurant. Tables filled the side of the room opposite the large, wooded bar. From another room, Beth could hear the crack of wood on wood from the bowling alley. Beth jumped at the sound.

"I take it you aren't a bowler," Marcus said with a smile, putting his hand on Beth's knee. "You'll get used to the noise."

"Beer?" the bartender asked Beth.

"Kevin," Marcus said before Beth could reply, "This is my friend, Beth. Beth, this is Kevin. He makes the best Old Fashioned in the county."

"It's a mix of Bourbon, bitters, and just the right amount of sugar and water," Kevin said, noting the confused look on Beth's face. "But you look more like a wine or daiquiri kind of girl."

Beth looked at Marcus for approval.

"You're not driving tonight," Marcus said, "Go for it."

"One strawberry daiquiri coming up," Kevin said as he turned away to make the drink.

"You want to sit at a table?" Marcus asked.

Beth nodded. This all felt odd and out of place. Whenever she had gone out before, Terry had done the deciding and the ordering. Beth could never imagine he would want to be seen in a place like this. Even in college he never went to the bars or commons area. And the bartender was right; it was always drinks like wine or champagne and top shelf at that.

Marcus and Chad helped her off the barstool and to the dining area. They pushed two tables together and sat down. MaryAnn and Richard, who Beth had met at Maifest, joined them.

"Are you ready to order?" a young girl around Aaron's age asked. "Or would you like a minute?"

"Give us a minute," Marcus said, "Unless you would like me to order for you, Beth"

Beth nodded again.

"Two chicken breast sandwiches with lettuce, tomato, and Swiss cheese, potato salad, and a basket of cheese curds."

Kevin brought over Beth's drink as the rest of the table ordered. Marcus again put his hand on Beth's knee and smiled.

"Is everything ok?" he asked, noticing Beth flinch slightly at the touch.

"It is all just a little overwhelming," Beth answered. "I feel out of place."

"You'll get used to it," Marcus said, patting her knee. "I think you will start to fit in real quick."

The conversation at the table quickly turned to the plans for the upcoming Fyr Bal Festival in Ephraim on Saturday. Beth listened intently to the reason behind the festival. She made note to learn more about the history later when she was back in her room. Right now, she listened more about how she would be helping MaryAnn with both the pancake breakfast and selling Edna's cherry pies to raise money for the Preservation Society. Beth also thought of the conversation she would have with Annie after the festival was over when she made their weekly Sunday phone call.

On the drive back to the inn, Marcus promised he would meet up after the ax throwing competition, something he had won or came in 2nd place for several years. Then he would take to her to the best spot to watch the fireworks.

Aaron sat silent in the back seat of the truck cab the entire ride back to the house without saying anything.

CHAPTER 21

Schools had been out for two weeks now, and that meant more business at the Bed and Breakfast. Beth had been asked to work longer hours and make multiple trips to the Piggly Wiggly for food. Her car had not yet been returned, so she had to depend on Aaron whose attitude had still not softened towards her. If Abby rode along, the tension wasn't as great but still evident.

Shifting the bag of eggs in her lap, Beth only paid half attention to Abby as she talked about going to nature camp in two weeks. It was near Milwaukee, and they would be going to the Zoo and some place called Holy Hill. Abby's excitement was contagious, and Beth found herself smiling at the constant chatter.

The truck stopped in the back driveway of the inn. Abby stayed in the truck as Beth carefully exited, balancing the bag of eggs and her purse. Aaron silently unloaded the rest of the groceries in three trips.

"Don't forget about tonight, Beth," Abby said over the slam of Aaron's truck door. "Marcus wants you to come over early for the meeting if you can."

"I'll try," Beth called out as the truck tires spun on the gavel of the drive.

As it turned out, Beth was so busy checking in guests that it was nearly 8:00 by the time she was able to cross through the archway gate dividing the backyard of the inn from Marcus's backyard. Even before she turned the corner of the garden shed, Beth could hear raised voices blending and talking over each other.

Marcus's estimate of 10-15 people attending this week's meeting proved to be horribly inaccurate. A quick glance told Beth there were about 40. The picnic tables were filled as well as the chairs on the deck. People had spread blankets on the grass and were sitting cross legged on the yard. Even the steps to the back door were filled.

Those who could not sit stood, drinking beer or soda, and munching on cookies Edna had sent over earlier in the day.

Beth stood in the background listening and trying to put names to faces. David was in his wheelchair wearing a brightly colored Superman t-shirt. Todd from the bakery in Jacksonport was there, and so was Kevin from the bar. Beth recognized others but still didn't know all the names. Edna was not going to be able to make it, and neither Aaron nor Abby was in the group. Beth was tempted to turn around and leave, but she knew she couldn't do that to Marcus who had asked her to be there.

"If we don't figure out some way to get that property," a loud voice Beth didn't recognize said. "Old man Ross and his big city cronies will swoop in and take it."

"That place hasn't been open for years" another man shouted, "It's an eyesore."

"But it's our eyesore," David shouted even louder than the others.

"So, you would rather have the Sunset replaced by an eyesore of a condo development?" Mrs. Wilson added.

"The whole point of tonight is preservation," Marcus began, "Protecting the things we love…" His statement was cut short as Kevin tapped him on the shoulder and pointed in Beth's direction. Marcus's stern expression melted into a smile.

"Take ten everyone," he said. "Cool off with a drink, and then we can begin again."

Beth walked closer to the crowd as Marcus stepped off the deck. He gave her a quick hug and whispered in her ear, "I was wondering when you would get here and save me from this mob of thugs."

CHAPTER 22

Beth yawned and looked at her watch. It was 10:00, a fact which a grandfather clock in the hallway verified with its loud chimes. Once the sun had started to set and the temperature dropped, most of the initial meeting goers had begun to leave and the dozen or so who chose to stay now gathered in Marcus's living room to have what Marcus called an 'organized discussion' on how to go about saving the Sunset.

David began the discussion.

"I have a friend at the historical society. She said, and this is making it sound less complicated than it is, if we can prove the history and ownership of the property, we may be able to petition the state to declare the Bar and Grill a historic landmark. We have to write a report as to the age of the property and why it is important to the area. Basically, what makes the property important enough to be called historic."

"How old does the property have to be?" Todd asked.

"Only 50 years, so even with the addition of the summer kitchen, this qualifies." David answered, checking his notes.

"You know how slow the wheels of government turn," Kevin said, "Do we have time to wait on a decision?"

"I agree," Mrs. Wilson chimed in. "I don't want to be the only one to point out the elephant in the room, but Miss Dickerson is 99 and had to go into assisted living. How much longer before she…" Mrs. Wilson shrugged her shoulders rather than finish that statement.

This brought more mutterings and comments from the group.

"Rather than sit around worrying about something that hasn't happened yet," Chad said, "We could start planning what to do if we can buy the property."

"How much is the property going to be?" a man Beth didn't recognize asked. "How much is 28 acres of waterfront property worth now? $1 million? $3 million? More?"

"And then you add on the repair costs," another person spoke up. "Not to mention the time and workers to do it all."

"We have to decide if saving the Sunset is really worth it," came a third opinion.

"I don't think we would all be here," Marcus said, standing up. "If we didn't feel this wouldn't be worth it."

"Rather than just talk, you need a plan," Beth said softly, surprised that she had the nerve to say anything. "You need to stop talking and start somewhere, anywhere."

"What was that?" David asked. "I can hardly hear you."

Beth took a deep breath.

"There needs to be a plan," Beth said, "Marcus already is looking into grants for the project. You do not need to come up with the money right away, and if you can tie up the sales proceedings."

"How do you think we can do that?" someone asked, his comment filled with sarcasm.

"She's right," Kevin said, coming to Beth's aid. "It's the government. Getting the state involved may take time. Like I said before, the wheels of bureaucracy turn slowly."

"But what about the money?" Mr. Dennis from the hardware store asked.

"Fundraisers," Beth replied, "This is the start of tourist season for all of you."

"It's going to take more than a few bake sales to raise a couple million dollars."

"Yes, it is," Todd said, rising to Beth's defense. "But like Beth said, it would be a start."

"Do you honestly think we would stand a chance against a big city developer?" the man who challenged Beth before asked, "We all have work to do. You said it yourself; this is tourist season."

More voices chimed in with complaints. Beth looked at Marcus. She could tell from the creases on his forehead Marcus was getting frustrated with the situation. David had apparently seen the same thing and angrily rapped his metal cane against his chair. Even Chad jumped at the sound.

"Let's let the little lady speak," David said, nodding in Beth's direction.

"All I am saying," Beth began, looking at David for support, "Is that sitting around a living room arguing is not going to solve anything. You talk and talk and talk about how important history is and how precious this land is, but no one seems willing to do anything but talk. I'm not saying that my ideas are perfect, or even very good for that matter, but if the Sunset Bar and Grill really is that important, shouldn't you at least try?"

Beth took in a deep breath and let it out in a sigh. She didn't believe she had the nerve to say all she had. As she noticed heads nodding in agreement and the smiles on Marcus's and David's faces, she felt better about her outburst.

"We need to start with a plan," David said.

"And a leader," Todd added.

"What about you, Marcus?" David asked.

"Oh, no," Marcus replied, "I have a hard time organizing my sock drawer. What about you, Mrs. Miller? If you can keep track of a class full of eighth graders, you can plan a few fundraisers."

"I have summer camp, and I need the time to unwind from said eighth graders," Mrs. Miller responded. "I am willing to help out though."

"What we need is someone who doesn't run a business in town," Chad said, a smile forming as his glance turned in Beth's direction. "Marcus said your car won't be ready for another week or so. Do you have anywhere to go after that?"

"Well, I…" Beth said with a stutter.

"You will be working for Edna all summer," Marcus said, coming over and putting his arm around Beth's shoulders.

"Then it's settled," Todd said standing up. "Everyone'll meet up Monday night at the Bowl at 7:00. I am sure Beth will have many great ideas to discuss then."

Beth leaned up against the table as Marcus went to help David down the deck ramp and watched as the rest of the guests dispersed. She took another big drink of her now warm lemonade.

"What just happened?" she asked, looking up as Marcus came back into the living room.

"My guess is you have been accepted to the neighborhood," Marcus replied.

Beth sighed again.

CHAPTER 23

"How was the meeting?" Edna called from the front room as Beth walked by.

"It went fine," Beth answered, not wanting to answer too many questions even though she had more than a few of her own. "I am really tired though. I am going to go up to bed."

"All right then, dear," Edna said, setting the book she had been reading on the table.

"I'll need your help for breakfast. Please be down by 6:00. We can talk then."

"I'll be down," Beth answered.

In her room, Beth undressed and set her alarm for 5:00. Even though there was a cool breeze coming in the window, Beth chose to leave it open, allowing the night sounds to filter into the room. The faint smell of wood smoke drifted into the room as well.

Beth picked up the desk phone and, just like last night, dialed the number. Instead of a recorded voice, Terry's groggy, "hello" greeted her.

Beth stood unable to speak.

Even when Terry repeated 'hello', she remained silent.

Beth quickly placed the phone back in the cradle and stood for a minute before crawling into bed.

CHAPTER 24

The ring of the telephone on the desk startled Beth awake. She had come back to her room shortly after cleaning the lunch dishes and started to work on more ideas for Monday's Sunset meeting and fell asleep in the chair. Beth blinked a few times and stared at the ringing phone. She had used the phone to call out, but never imagined anyone would ever call in. On the fifth ring, she picked up the receiver.

"Hello?"

"Well, it's about time you answered," came Marcus's voice from the other end of the line.

"What do you want and how did you know I would be in my room?"

"Last question first," Marcus replied, "I called downstairs, and Samantha connected me. As for the first rude question, I was finished fixing the stair lift at the church and thought I would come and take you to Wilson's for ice cream."

"Again, with the ice cream," Beth said with a grin. "What are you trying to do, fatten me up?"

"I just wanted an excuse to see you, and ice cream seemed as good an excuse as any."

"As nice as your offer is, I am going to have to refuse," Beth said. "Edna and Samantha are going shopping this afternoon, and I am watching the Inn and baby Lynette."

"Well then," Marcus replied, determined not to be refused, "If you can't go out for ice cream, the ice cream will have to come to you."

"I can accept that," Beth said.

"You have to. I insist. See you in about half an hour then."

Beth stared at the phone for a moment, then hung up. She didn't know why, but she felt like a giddy schoolgirl Abby's age.

After a quick shower, Beth changed into a pair of jeans she had picked up at the thrift store. With the lower ride around her waist and hips and a slight flare at the ankles, the jeans gave her a neat, slim look. Choosing a top was another matter altogether. The blue button down was too stuffy. Her yellow print top was too low cut, she decided and tossed the blouse on the bed next to the other three she had discarded. She finally decided on the red capped sleeve with the little bow. It was neither too tight nor too loose.

Beth surveyed her look in the mirror. Pulling her still damp hair back in a ponytail, she noticed the glint of gold peeking out from the neckline of her top. Beth reached up and carefully undid the chain's clasp and slipped the chain, rings and all, into her jeans pocket.

"Beth," Edna called up the stairs. "Marcus is here."

Beth checked her look in the mirror one last time.

Beth smiled when she saw Marcus at the bottom of the steps next to Edna, a heaping cup of ice cream in each hand.

"You two have a nice afternoon," Edna said on her way out the door. "And Beth, I won't be needing you tonight, so if you have plans…"

When she saw the incredibly large grin on Marcus's face, Beth knew Edna had purposely left that sentence unfinished.

CHAPTER 25

"So," Beth said, taking another bite of broasted chicken from the picnic basket. "How long were you and Edna talking this morning before Samantha transferred the call?"

"What makes you think I was talking with Edna?" Marcus replied. "You think I can't plan a picnic on my own?"

"I recognize the basket and the napkins. I helped pack plenty of these for guests."

"You caught me," Marcus said with a laugh, wiping peach juice from his chin. "The important thing is, are you enjoying your surprise?"

Beth smiled and nodded.

"I am, and it gives me a chance to better get to know your son. Maybe get him to like me a bit more."

The wind picked up, shaking the leaves on the tree. Marcus grabbed for the napkins threatening to blow off the table.

"Are you cold?" Marcus asked.

"What gave me away? My chattering teeth or the fact that my goosebumps are growing to the size of small mountains?"

Marcus turned toward the playground,

"Aaron. Abby," he called out. "Can you please grab the sweaters out of the back seat?"

"Right away," Abby answered.

"You brought a sweater for me, too?" Beth asked, caught off guard by the kind gesture.

"Samantha took it from your closet this morning while cleaning rooms."

"I thought this was supposed to be summer," Beth said, slipping her arms into the sweater Abby held out to her. "Feels more like fall."

"This is Door County," Aaron said sarcastically. "Give it five minutes."

"We had snowflakes on July 4th one day," Abby said with a laugh. "At least that's what mom said."

"You are just not accustomed to lakeside weather," Marcus said. "You have city blood. You need to be full of good, strong German blood like me." Marcus emphasized the last words with a fist thump on his chest.

"That's not all you are full of," Beth said, smiling.

Abby and Aaron began picking up the plates and covering the leftover food. Aaron popped open another bottle of root beer and sat down on the picnic table. He took out a pocketknife and began carving on a piece of wood he had picked up from the ground after taking the picnic basket to the car.

"I'll be right back," Marcus said, heading in the direction of the bathroom.

"I gotta go, too," Abby said, skipping after him, leaving Beth and Aaron alone at the picnic table.

"What are you making?" Beth asked, looking over Aaron's shoulder.

"A bird," Aaron replied not looking up.

"Do you carve other things?"

"Sometimes. Grandpa showed me," Aaron said with a shrug.

"You do not like me much, do you?"

"You're ok."

"It is fine if you don't," Beth said, "but since I am going to be around for a while and working with your dad, it would be nice to get to know each other a little bit."

"Yeah, ok."

"Yeah, ok," Beth replied.

"Hey, Beth," Abby called, running back from the bathroom, "you gotta see this cool rock I found."

"Let me see," Beth replied. "It is pretty cool."

Abby held out the cream-colored rock with black splotches.

"I have a collection in my room," Abby said proudly, "I'm going to be a geologist when I go to college, or an archaeologist."

"That is very ambitious", Beth replied.

"I know," Abby said, standing up straighter, a large smile on her face.

Several seagulls circled overhead and more walked around the picnic area squawking and looking for scraps. A group of teenagers pulled into the parking lot and began an impromptu game of flag football. Aaron and Abby waved to them and joined in on the game, leaving Beth and Marcus alone with the seagulls.

"This place is beautiful," Beth said, staring out over the waters of Lake Michigan. "So blue and huge."

"It is the best park in the county," Marcus said, "at least I think so. This was one of Sarah's favorite places. We would pack a picnic lunch and Sarah's art supplies and come here at least once a month. Then when Aaron came along, we brought him here, too. He would bring his crayons and finger paints and color alongside his mother. After his mother died, Aaron refused to even come near here. That is until Abby came along."

"Edna said they were close," Beth said.

"I think Abby is the baby sister Aaron always wanted to have."

Just then another wind gust blew up, sending the gulls flying and the waves off Lake Michigan beating against the cliffs with a loud whoosh.

"Oh, good," Marcus said, taking Beth's hand, I was hoping the wind would pick up. Let me show you what makes this place so special."

Marcus walked Beth over towards the edge of the water as another wave crashed into the limestone hollow sending water shooting into the air and onto the path in front of them. Beth jumped back to avoid getting wet.

"I am really afraid of heights," she said, "Do we have to get so close?"

"Now, you trust me, don't you?" Marcus asked, taking Beth by both hands.

"I am not so sure now," Beth answered, nervously.

"I am your rescuer, remember. Now, close your eyes and step with me."

Beth carefully shuffled her feet across the pathway and over a small tree root Marcus warned her about.

"Another big wave is coming in," Marcus whispered. "Keep your eyes closed. Just feel."

Beth let out a startled cry as she heard and felt the crash under her feet.

"What was that?"

"These cliffs are all limestone," Marcus explained. "Over the ages, the waves have worn the limestone into caves. What you are feeling are the waves hitting underneath us. It is quite amazing how powerful the water can be. Do you want to get closer?"

"I think I am high enough for one night."

"This isn't high," Marcus replied, "Just wait until I take you to Eagle Tower Observation tower. That is high."

"You wouldn't dare."

"You wanted the Door County experience, didn't you."

Beth let out a small whimper as another wave crashed on the shore, catching Beth off guard, making her step back against the tree root she had just avoided, sending her careening sideways. She would have fallen had Marcus not been quick enough to catch her under her arms. He held her in his arms for a minute before setting her back on her feet.

Beth looked up at Marcus and smiled.

"I told you *you* could trust me," Marcus said, returning the smile.

Behind them Aaron scowled at the pair and let out an annoyed grunt. Abby, a big smile on her face, reached out and backhandedly slapped Aaron on the shoulder. Aaron grunted again and started back towards the car.

CHAPTER 26

"What was that?" Annie asked, as another loud boom sounded over the bay. Beth had put her cellphone speaker on while she rocked and fed baby Lynette on the porch facing the west. Over the trees she could just barely see the lights of high shooting fireworks. The sounds echoed across the bay with a short delay. Lynette seemed not to mind as long as Beth kept swinging.

"Fyr Bal down in Ephraim," Beth replied.

"And that means what?"

"Sorry," Beth said with a laugh. "I forgot I didn't tell you last time we talked. Fyr Bal is a Scandinavian festival they hold up here for the solstice. The shores of Ephraim are lined with bonfires in the symbolic burning of the winter witch."

"So, another reason to have fun up there? Did ya sell corndogs again?"

"Pancakes and pies this time."

"You're steppin' up," Annie said. "Next you are gonna tell me you did the cookin' of the pancakes."

"We want people to buy the food…"

"Rather than pay you not to cook it?" Annie finished the sentence, perhaps not in the way Beth had meant.

"You are so mean. True, but mean."

"I gotta be me."

"I miss you," Beth said quietly, "I wish you were here so I could share this place with you. I know you would like it. The kids, too. You wouldn't believe Lake Michigan. It is nothing like Barker Meadow. No matter how you look at it, you can't see the other shore, and it is so blue green. Marcus took me there on a picnic the other night."

"Just the two of you?"

"No, Aaron and Abby came along, but it was still nice."

"So, did ya kiss him yet?"

"Annie!"

"Well, did ya?"

"No."

"What cha waitin' for?" Annie said in mock disgust. "You've been there a month. Git your act together."

"I am not ready to jump into anything," Beth replied "I am just enjoying being free for a change. I did do something, though."

"What?"

"I took the rings off and put them in a drawer," Beth said slowly.

"Oh my gosh, girl," Annie said, surprised and pleased at the same time. "How'd that feel?"

"Scary, weird, liberating," Beth admitted. "After 25 years, I felt naked. If I can be honest, guilty."

"Why?"

"I wonder if I should have been more understanding about Terry's work. I mean, he was doing the extra hours for us."

"He was doin' it for himself first," Annie corrected Beth, "There were plenty of times he could've and should've said no. Your anniversary for one."

"But he…"

"No buts girl!" Annie shot back, "Ya wanna know what that jerk did this week? He called the cops. They came to the house and the salon. Scared the kids. He still thinks I'm hidin' ya from him."

Annie's angry words scared Lynette who started to cry and squirm on Beth's lap.

"Shh baby," Beth said, placing Lynette gently upright against her shoulder and patting her back to soothe her. "Annie didn't mean to yell."

"I did to mean to yell," Annie replied, "But not scare a baby." Annie took a breath. "Wait, you got a baby?"

"She's not mine," Beth said softly, "She's Samantha's. I'm just babysitting for the night."

Samantha knocked on Beth's door and took Lynette to their room.

Beth changed into her pajamas and settled into bed with Annie's voice and over a dozen fundraising ideas swirling in her head.

"Today was a good day," Beth thought as she drifted off to sleep.

CHAPTER 27

Kevin had Beth's strawberry daiquiri waiting for her by the time she had unloaded everything from Marcus's truck and set up in the Bowl.

"I may need more than one of these tonight, Kevin," Beth said, as she surveyed the crowd gathered in the dining room. If she thought the crowd at Marcus's last week was big, this gathering was twice the size at least. Beth took a drink of her cocktail and followed it up with a large nervous sigh.

"You sigh a lot," Marcus said, stepping in from behind Beth and putting his hands on her shoulders. "Just think of it. All these people are here waiting for you."

"That is not helping one bit," Beth said nervously.

"You will do great," Marcus replied, "Just tell it like you practiced with me. The only difference is that instead of just me, you have about a hundred more eyes staring at you. How much harder is that?"

"Definitely not helping!" Beth said, sighing again. "I thought you were my friend."

"I am just keeping it real, as Aaron would say. I can leave if you don't want me here," Marcus said, setting his beer on the bar and pretending to move away.

"You wouldn't dare!" Beth said, grabbing Marcus's arm. "You got me into this mess; you are staying right here."

"If I remember correctly, it was Todd who nominated you."

"But you agreed to it."

"I heard my name over here," Todd said, appearing seemingly out of nowhere. "Beth, Marcus, this is Chris, David's friend from the historical society."

Chris put out his hand and accepted Marcus's return shake.

"David was unable to make it tonight, so I offered to introduce Chris to everyone," Todd explained.

"I hope you don't mind my being forward," Chris said, taking Beth's hand between both of his and offering a quick brush of a kiss on Beth's cheek, "David explained your situation, and I went ahead and did some research. All the needed papers have been ordered, and the ball is started to roll for declaring the Sunset a historical landmark."

"Tha… thank you," Beth stammered, not knowing if she was more caught off guard by the research or the kiss.

"He does that to everyone," Todd said, leaning in and whispering in Beth's ear. "Chris is mostly harmless."

Beth looked up in Marcus's direction and noticed the scowl on his face. She also noticed he wasn't looking at her and Chris but in the direction of the door.

"What is he doing here?" Marcus said with disgust. "Shows up like a little cockroach."

Beth followed Marcus's gaze, as did Chris's and Todd's. Seated solo at a table by the entrance was Carlson Ross, flicking open and shut his ever-present lighter.

It only took a few angry strides, and Marcus was standing at Carlson's table.

"You can't smoke here, you know," Marcus said, still scowling.

"Do you see any cigarettes?" Carlson shot back. "I don't. So, I suggest you find someone else to harass."

"I don't recall anyone inviting you here," Marcus said, not backing down.

"It's a public meeting and a public space," Carlson said calmly. "It was in the Pulse. The notice said concerned citizens welcome, and I am a citizen the last time I looked."

"Let him stay," Chad, in full sheriff deputy uniform, said, stepping through the door, "Just wipe that smirk off your face, Ross. And no trouble."

"I wouldn't dream of it, deputy, sir," Carlson answered back, "I am now going to go up to the bar and get a drink. I have my ID if you want to card me."

The bell on the wall next to the bar clanged loudly, cutting off any reply Chad may have wanted to snap back with.

"Quiet down everyone," Fred Wickman shouted over the noise in the bar. "I don't have my gavel tonight so the bell will have to do." He rang it again, this time softer than the first time.

Muffled laughter filled the room as those people milling around found places to sit or in many cases stand. Beth looked over at Marcus who had come back over to join her. She noticed Marcus was keeping a close eye on Carlson, who had taken his old-fashioned back to his table and began knuckle-rolling his lighter between his fingers.

"For those who have not met her yet," Fred continued, "I would like to introduce you to Beth Campbell. Beth is staying up at the Rose for the summer to help Edna while Samantha is caring for her new baby. I am happy to say, Beth has agreed to lead the fundraising campaign for the restoration of the Sunset."

Cheers, applause, and whistles from the crowd caused Beth to blush and shrink back against the bar a bit.

"Don't be shy," Fred said, extending a hand out to Beth, "Come up here and join me."

Beth looked nervously at Marcus who silently mouthed "go on."

Beth smiled back and approached the front of the bar to stand next to Fred.

"I hear from Marcus you have been spending many a late night planning some events," Fred said to Beth. "Please, share them with the rest of the class."

Fred's carefully phrased remark to help Beth relax was met with the desired soft laughter, and Beth took a deep breath.

"Thank you, Mr. Wickman," Beth said tentatively.

"Since we're working together," Fred corrected, "Call me Fred."

Beth smiled again, beginning to feel more comfortable. She reached for the portable whiteboard resting next to the bar and opened it. On the board, complete with bullet points, numbers, and color coding was Beth's well laid plans.

"First we will need to know how much money we need to shoot for," Beth said, indicating the board. "We have to find a contractor for an estimate on the cost of repairs. That will also involve finding an inspector to make sure everything that needs fixing can even be fixed. Then there is the cost of the property itself."

For the next hour, Beth continued laying out what she had been working on. Marcus watched as Beth introduced Chris and let him speak regarding the historical property process.

Between the two of them, they fielded questions and listened to concerns. During that time, the enthusiasm in the room was flowing as easily as the beers and drinks. Beth noticed that even Carlson Ross had stopped fidgeting with his lighter and was listening intently.

At 9:30, Fred rang the bell and suggested everyone should go home, think about what had been talked about, and plan to meet at Waterfront Park the following Sunday night if they wanted to help.

It was after 10:00 by the time everyone had filtered out. Beth's face was hurting from smiling, and she was tired from shaking hands and being hugged by many of the women, something 'she would have to get used to,' Todd informed her.

The ride back to the Inn was quiet mainly because Beth was too tired to talk. Respecting her silence, Marcus reached over to brush the loose strands of hair off Beth's face before reaching on her lap and twining his fingers around hers. Beth did not turn her head to look at Marcus but instead kept her gaze on the road.

After they had parked at the back parking area behind the Inn, Marcus walked to Beth's side of the truck and helped her down to the ground.

"You did really good tonight," Marcus said, placing his hands on Beth's shoulders gently. Looking Beth straight in the eyes, he continued softly, "I'm proud of you."

"Really?" Beth asked, not having anyone but her mother and Annie tell her that before.

"Really," Marcus replied, smiling.

Beth returned the smile.

The two of them stood silent under the dim light of the waning moon and yellow back porch light.

Still holding onto Beth's shoulder, Marcus bent down and gently kissed Beth first on the forehead, and after a beat, on the lips.

Beth took in a quick startled breath, then relaxed into the kiss.

CHAPTER 28

"You are working yourself way too hard, my dear," Edna said, bringing Beth a tray containing a ham and Swiss sandwich, fresh-made potato salad, and sliced apple. "You are going to wear yourself out with this fundraiser plan of yours."

"There is just so much to get ready for before Thursday," Beth answered. "I thought the parades were Saturday."

"Unfortunately for you, no. Is there anything I can help you with?"

"Short of stopping time or finding some mice or birds or even a fairy godmother to wave a magic wand and get these flyers finished, I don't think so."

"I don't think I can do that," Edna said laughing. "But I can provide an unending supply of iced tea."

"That would be nice too," Beth replied.

"All right then," Edna said going back into the house singing "Bibbidi-Bobbidi-Boo,"

Beth sat back in the patio change and reached for the sandwich. Cleo jumped up into her lap and let out a short meow.

"No, you can't have my sandwich, you little beggar," Beth said gently. "Don't look at me with those eyes."

Cleo meowed again and brushed his head against Beth's arm.

"Oh, all right, but just this once," Beth said, pulling a small piece of ham from the sandwich and giving it to the cat. Cleo made short work of the meat and looked up for more.

"One piece is all you get."

Cleo meowed again.

"If I meow, will you feed me ham," Marcus asked, coming up the porch steps.

"I didn't know you were coming over today," Beth said, not looking up.

"I was finished with setting up the picnic tables at the park and thought I would see if you needed anything."

"No, not really," Beth replied.

"The fliers look great," Marcus said, coming closer to the tables. "Dan said if I get them over to him today, he will print up 1000 of them by morning."

"That's good."

"The YMCA camp kids did a nice job decorating the float."

"I will have to see that on Thursday."

"And the candy is all in buckets for handing out at both parades."

"I will cross that off the list," Beth said, moving over in the chair a few inches as Marcus came closer.

"Do you want to ride up front with me for the parades?" Marcus asked, noticing Beth's shift and Cleo jumping off her lap.

"I think I should sit in the back of the float and help refill the candy buckets," Beth replied.

"Is there anything else?"

"Just let me put this flyer on the flash drive and then you can take it to be printed."

"That's all you need?"

"Yes"

"Is everything ok?" Marcus asked, noticing that Beth had not even looked up in his direction since he came up on the porch, just stared at the laptop on the table. Even when she pulled the flash drive out of the laptop, Beth had only placed it on the table and slid it in Marcus's direction.

"Hello Marcus," Edna said cheerfully, coming onto the porch. "I didn't know you were coming over."

"I finished my work early and came to see if I could help with anything here," Marcus replied, taking the pitcher of iced tea from Edna and giving her a quick peck on the head.

Beth took this opportunity to excuse herself and went into the house without saying a word.

"Did something happen between you two," Edna asked, noting the concerned look on Marcus's face as he watched Beth leave. "I thought you two were getting along just fine."

"So did I," Marcus replied, "We had a good time at the picnic. The meeting on Monday was a success. Then when I dropped her back here, we had a short talk. Everything was good until I kissed her goodnight."

"Oh," Edna said quietly, "I see."

Marcus looked over at Edna, who was now facing the door Beth had used to enter the house.

CHAPTER 29

Beth pulled the rocking chair up next to the open window in her room and took a deep breath of the crisp night air. After the sun had set, the temperature had dropped into the low 60's, a contrast to the high 70's and bright sun during the parades in Baileys Harbor and Egg Harbor earlier in the day. Even though she had ridden on the back of the float pulled by Marcus and Aaron, the sun and fresh air had made her tired. It wasn't until she had felt the pulsing water of the shower hitting her skin did she realize how, even with sunscreen, she had managed to burn her bare arms, shoulders, and legs. Her hat had prevented a burn on her face, though.

Taking a bite of peach pie picked up at Sweetie Pie's, a traditional stop after the parades according to Aaron, Beth listened to Annie's children's voices on the answering machine followed by the beep.

"Annie," Beth said into the phone, her voice shaking, "I know you are out with the kids tonight, but please call me. I really need to talk to you tonight."

Beth hung up the phone and rested her head against the back of the chair. With one hand, she rubbed the thin gold chain between her fingers.

Cleo let out a soft mew and jumped up on Beth's lap nearly knocking the pie to the floor. Beth caught the plate before it fell, her wedding rings clinking against the china.

"Hey you," Beth said, addressing the cat who was now curling up on her lap and setting the plate on the table. "Did you have a good day?"

Cleo looked up at Beth and meowed again, his eyes soft and attentive.

"You are so lucky to be a cat," Beth said, stroking Cleo's back and tail. "All you have to worry about is who is going to feed you and pet you and bring you fresh catnip."

Another meow.

Outside the window came the jarring pops of firecrackers and sparklers, which sent Cleo jumping off Beth's lap to the safe space under the dresser. The smell of a campfire wafted in with the breeze accompanied by the bitter smell of firecrackers. Laughter and voices echoed in from outside. Rising above the other voices, Beth could pick out Marcus' deep laugh.

Beth quickly stood up, turned off the bedside lamp, and pulled her curtains closed before burying herself under the sheet and light bedspread. She buried her face in the pillow feeling her face become warm and tears form in her eyes. She wound the necklace chain around her wrist before falling into an uneasy sleep.

CHAPTER 30

Beth was startled awake at 1:00 when her cell phone trilled with Annie's familiar ring.

"What's the SOS, hon?" Annie asked, "Sorry it took so long. The kids and me were up in the mountains in a dead zone, or I would've called sooner. Is it Terry?"

"No, not Terry," Beth answered, wiping the sleep from her eyes. "It's me."

"Are you ok?"

"Yes. No. I don't know."

"Clearly you're not," Annie said, "What's goin' on?"

"I did something, Annie. Something bad." Beth's voice quivered as she blinked back the tears that threatened to start.

"What? Just tell me."

"Marcus," Beth choked out. "Marcus kissed me."

"Oh my gosh, Beth, that's great. About time too."

Beth said nothing but rather let the tears fall.

"That is great?" Annie asked, "Ain't it?"

"I…I don't know," Beth replied. "It was nice, but…"

"But what?"

"I kissed him back."

"And?"

"Annie," Beth answered, her breathing hard and labored, "Annie, I kissed Marcus back. I cheated on my husband."

There was silence on the phone line as Annie took in Beth's words.

Beth slipped the chain with her rings back around her neck.

"I did the one thing I was afraid he was doing to me," Beth said shakily, breaking the silence. "I cheated. I broke the marriage vows."

"Oh sweetie," Annie said softly, "You may have kissed Marcus, but Terry cheated on you first. He chose to leave you first, not for a person, but his job and his boss and himself."

"But our marriage…"

"Your marriage was over long before this. You said it yourself. All that's left is the paperwork."

"But…"

"But nothin'," Annie said, her voice firm and calm, "I've been down this road twice before. Has he called? No. He thinks you are just having a fit and will come back when you get bored, and the money runs out."

"Maybe I should come home."

"Don't you dare!" Annie said, her usual calm tone fading into anger and frustration, "That's exactly what he wants you to do. Give up. You're better than that. And you deserve better than Terry."

"Annie," Beth said, her voice cracking and tears flowing down her cheeks. "What am I supposed to do?"

"I know what I would do, and it would involve duct tape, rope and a shovel, but I'm not you," Annie said, "What I do know is you can't undo the kiss or the feelings that let that kiss happen. Now, go back to bed and get yourself some sleep."

"I don't think I can sleep," Beth said.

"Go lay down," Annie said again. "Take a few deep breaths."

Beth did as she was told, too mentally exhausted to argue.

"Now," Annie said quietly. "What else do ya need, besides some good wine and even better chocolate?"

"Stay with me," Beth replied, resting her head on the pillow.

"As long as you need," Annie said. "What else?"

"Talk to me."

"What about?"

"Anything. Nothing."

"Jimmy hit a home run at the softball game today," Annie said quietly.

"That must have been something to see," Beth said, turning the phone's speaker on and placing it next to her on the pillow.

"And Bri got accepted to UNLV as a hospitality major."

"She always did have a dream of working on a cruise ship," Beth said.

"And gettin' paid to see the world," Annie said, finishing the statement.

"Annie…"

"Yeah?"

"Thanks," Beth said, taking another deep breath, "Please keep talking."

"Anythin' for you, hon," Annie said. "I got a new client at the salon. Mrs. Francine LaViolett, with two t's. She's a real snob, but she tips real good. And the creepy guy from the coffee shop is still coming in, tryin' to hit on Cassie even though she's now seven months pregnant and big as a house…"

Annie's stories continued until rhythmic breathing indicated Beth had fallen asleep.

"You'll know what to do, you always do," Annie said quietly and hung up the phone.

CHAPTER 31

Sunday morning flew by in a blur. The July 4th revelers seemed eager to check out and leave for the long and congested drive back to Chicago or Minneapolis or places further south. Beth and Samantha had packed more boxed breakfasts and lunches than they served in the dining area, and Edna had booked her fair share of returning visitors for the following year. The three of them, with Abby's help, had stripped the rooms in record time. With only half of the rooms needing to be straightened for Monday, Edna had excused Beth with instructions to work on the plans for that night's picnic.

Beth had gladly taken Edna up on her kind offer and took her planning book, white boards, and ledger out to the side porch to be out of the sun and nearly 80-degree heat. Cleo was curled in his basket in the shade and from time to time would dip a front paw into the water bowl next to him and splash himself with the ice cube cooled water.

"Yes, Mrs. Miller," Beth said into the phone she was holding between her shoulder and cheek, "I have collected all the canisters from Ellison Bay on up to Northport and emptied them. MonaRae is collecting the ones from the Island, and then her and Helga and Dorothy will be counting those."

Beth paused, listening to Mrs. Miller's line of questions.

"I am sure there will be plenty of replacement canisters to hand out tonight. Between your camp kids and the scout troops, we have at least 50 more empties."

More silence on Beth's part.

"Yes, I will let you know if we need more. Chris was able to get more of the pictures of the old Sunset printed off and cut."

Another pause.

"Yes, I will bring them tonight. And the unfinished cans and pictures. Thank you, Mrs. Miller, I mean Julie, I will see you tonight around 6:30."

"For someone who said she was too busy to help out much," Beth said, hanging up the phone and placing it upside down on the table, "She has a lot to say. Wouldn't you agree, Lynette?"

Baby Lynette cooed from her bassinet.

"Beth," Abby called from inside the house, "Edna needs you in the back yard."

"Right now?" Beth asked back, "I have the baby out here with me."

"I'm coming to watch her," Abby answered stepping onto the porch, "Edna says it's important."

"Well, if Edna says it is important, I guess I better go," Beth said with a smile, "Just stay out of my kolaches," she added, seeing Abby reaching for the plate.

When Beth made it to the back yard, she expected to see Edna with a basket full of fresh vegetables from the garden. Instead, there was Marcus and Aaron and Edna talking to a man she had never seen before talking and laughing. Beth paused when she saw Marcus and brushed the crumbs from her jeans and straightened her shoulders.

"Abby said you needed to see me," Beth called out to the group. "She said it was important."

Edna and Marcus turned towards her, both with large smiles on their faces. Marcus was holding something up in the air. As she approached, Beth recognized the blue and orange Peacock keychain.

"Betty!" she shouted, picking up her pace and holding out her hand for the keychain.

"You've got one sweet car there," the man Beth didn't recognize said.

When Beth looked up from her car, she noticed the name Keith on his shirt.

"I haven't seen too many of these original VW's with less than 100,000 miles on them and in such good shape," Keith continued, "You sure took good care of her."

"She was in the garage for most of the last 25 years," Beth answered, gently touching her car. "Thank you for fixing her."

"It was my pleasure. I wish I could have finished her sooner, but the parts are not the easiest to find up here."

"That's ok. She is back now," Beth answered, turning now to face Keith and Marcus.

"How much do I owe you?"

"Nothing," Keith said, "It's all paid for."

"What?" Beth asked, confused.

"The repairs have been paid for," Edna said, putting a hand on Beth's shoulder.

"You didn't do that, did you?" Beth asked Edna,

"Not me," Edna said as she turned toward Marcus who was getting into his truck along with Keith and Aaron. "I had nothing to do with paying for the repairs."

Beth, keychain held tightly in her hand against her chest, watched as the truck turned around and left the driveway, and mouthed a silent, "Thank you."

CHAPTER 32

Beth allowed her head to sink into the soft pillow on the porch swing. The front porch overlooking the road offered a view of the water during the daylight hours. At this time of night, since it was after midnight, Beth was only able to hear the waves hitting the rocks and catch a glimpse of green and red lights from a few sailboats still out on the bay. The lapping of the waves and the slight squeak of the porch swing were having the desired relaxing effect Beth was looking for. Marcus had offered many times to 'desqueak' the swing, but Edna had always refused. "The swing has squeaked ever since Earl hung it. Why fix it now?"

The sound of a car pulling up in front of the house startled Beth to reality. She squinted, attempting to see who the person was who had stepped out of the car and was now approaching the front steps. A momentary panic set in thinking Terry had somehow found out where she had gone to and was now coming to drag her back to Colorado.

"You're up late," Chad said, stepping up onto the porch.

"I could say the same about you," Beth replied, relieved at seeing who was stopping in this late. "I thought you might be a late tourist looking for a room."

"Nope," Chad said with a laugh, "Those only show up on people's lawns in the middle of thunderstorms."

"Do not remind me," Beth replied, "That was a night to forget. Even if the results were not all that bad. But seriously, why are you stopping here so late."

"Kind of a slow night with half the tourists gone back home. I wanted to see if Marcus was up, but his house is dark."

"He and Aaron came home about an hour ago. They went straight into the house."

"So, Aaron was with him?"

"Yes, they were both talking and laughing about something. Then, like I said, they went into the house."

"Hmm."

"Why does that 'hmm' sound like there is something behind it?" Beth asked.

"I got a call earlier about some kids breaking into the fireworks shack by the gas station just north of Fish Creek. Cameras picked up a car matching Wade Kole's car, but we couldn't see the plates. I wanted to find out if Aaron was hanging around Wade or the other boys tonight."

"Marcus told me Aaron was planning on helping with the fish boils all night," Beth replied. "So, I don't think so. Was anything stolen?"

"Mostly smoke bombs and a few sparklers," Chad replied. "The worker that came over didn't think anything else was taken, but he seemed a little nervous. He didn't want to file a formal report either, which usually means there were some not so legal fireworks under the counter."

"Do you want me to ask Marcus in the morning?"

"I'll stop by at the end of shift. He's usually awake by then," Chad said with a slight shrug. "There's nothing I can really do without a complaint. I just don't like loose ends."

"I understand that part," Beth said, holding back a yawn.

"Don't start that," Chad replied, stifling a yawn of his own. "I have six more hours to go."

"Sorry," Beth said with a laugh. "I am usually in bed by now. I have to start work when you are getting off."

"Have a good night then," Chad said, heading back to his car.

Chad stopped halfway to his car and turned back towards Beth.

"I hear you have Betty back," he said.

"Yes, I do," Beth replied. "And the bill was all paid for, too."

"That's good. I hope having your car back helps," Chad said. "You have a good night now."

"You, too," Beth replied.

Beth stood on the porch watching the Sheriff car drive off heading north.

Not bothering to hold back yet another yawn, Beth collected her sweater off the swing and went into the house.

CHAPTER 33

Beth could smell brats and burgers cooking at the park even before she was parked. There had to be more than two dozen cars lining the road, however. As she approached, she saw Abby and her friend Angel standing in a parking spot and waving her down.

"Hi girls," Beth said through the open window. "Can you find a few more helpers to unload the car?"

Even before she had all the words out, Abby and Angel were sprinting off in the direction of the pavilion and quickly returned with two more helpers.

"Thank you, Betty," Beth whispered, stroking the steering wheel. Even though the trip had been short, being behind the wheel again felt so satisfying. There was such a difference between choosing not to drive and not being able to drive or allowed to drive. The feeling of freedom Beth had experienced in May washed over her again, and Beth rested her head against the back of the seat, closed her eyes, and listened to the sounds of laughter and children playing.

"We're back," Abby said in her familiar sing-song voice.

Beth opened the truck and handed out boxes and tote bags to the waiting hands of the kids Abby had brought over to help.

"Careful with the bowls," she said, as she watched Angel take the potato salad out of the back seat. "They were on ice so the bowls might be wet."

It took only one more trip and a handful of teens to get Betty unloaded and everything carried to the pavilion.

"Hello Beth," Chris said, giving Beth the now familiar cheek kiss. "How is the canister collection going?"

"We have cans all over the peninsula," Beth answered, pulling an empty out of the box and handing it to him. "Your photos are getting a great deal of attention, which helps."

"Glad I could be of service," Chris replied, taking the can, "If you need anything else, just ask."

"I will keep that in mind," Beth said. "There are a few other events I am going to need help with before all this fundraising is over."

"Beth, Chris, over here," Kevin called from a table, "We saved you a spot."

Beth looked over and saw Kevin, Chad, and Marcus sitting together, plates of food and drinks in front of them. Todd was arriving at the table with a large plate of watermelon and took one of the empty spaces on the table as well.

"I thought you two would like to sit on the ends," Marcus said, standing up at their approach. "It will be easier when you have to stand up and speak."

Marcus had a slight smile and glint in his eye as he spoke, as if he had a secret.

"What?" Beth asked Marcus.

"You'll find out soon enough," Marcus replied. "Would you like me to get you a plate?"

"I can do it myself," Beth answered.

"I need to see what goodies Edna sent along before the kids eat them all," he said, holding his hand out to help Beth up from the table. Beth followed Marcus, not taking his outstretched hand.

When they were out of earshot of the others, Marcus began to speak quietly,

I'm sorry, Beth, I wasn't thinking the other night," he confessed. "It had been such a good night, and well."

"I wasn't prepared for that," Beth said, picking up an ear of corn out of the salted butter pan with the tongs and putting it on her plate.

"Edna filled me in," Marcus said, adding a brat to Beth's plate. "I'm a little out of practice reading lady clues."

"Can we just forget about it?" Beth asked, reaching for the coleslaw.

"Forget about what?" Marcus jokingly replied.

"Exactly," Beth said, adding a piece of blueberry cobbler to Marcus's plate.

Beth looked up at Marcus and smiled weakly. Deep down she wasn't really sure if she was ready to forget yet, and the rings around her neck were a reminder of that.

Beth took a cup of cheese curds, a bun with sauerkraut, and went back over to the picnic table with Marcus following.

"Good evening, everyone," Fred Wickman's voice called out from the front table where he was standing. "I know you are all here to have a good time and enjoy some delicious food, but, as you know there is still a lot of work to be done for the Sunset restoration project."

Applause from the gathered group.

"I also know there is some good news from the state," Fred continued. "Christopher, would you like to stand up and share your news with us, please?"

Chris stood to more applause and whistles.

"Thank you all," he said waving at the group. "As you know, I have a dear friend at the state historical society. I bribed her with cheese curds and a fish boil, and she was able to fast-track a visit up here on Wednesday to tour the property."

Cheers and excited talking followed up Chris's words.

"Does this mean we were approved?"

"Who is all coming?"

"What will all this cost?"

All these questions and more overlapped, the excitement evident in their tones.

"One question at a time, please," Chris shouted over the din. "No, we have not yet been approved. This is simply preliminary. Barb is coming to interview Ruby Dickerson, tour the property, and check out any other records available."

"How much will this cost?" Bennie Jefferson asked from his table.

"Nothing for this visit except the cost for dinner," Chris responded with a laugh. "I have also made arrangements with Edna for Barb to stay at The Rose's Tuesday night since that is where Beth and all the fundraising information is. When you see Edna, please, thank her for this kindness."

"Thank you, Christopher," Fred said, quieting the applause that had broken out. "If you have any more questions, I am sure Christopher will be happy to answer them if he has more information."

Chris nodded in agreement.

"Now, on to the really important part, how much have we raised so far," Fred said. "Beth, this is your time to shine."

Beth took a sip of her root beer before walking up to the front table, money canister and ledger papers in hand.

"First of all," Beth said, holding up the canister, "I would like to thank Chris for these beautiful canisters. There are more than 340 of these up and down the peninsula. They would not be possible without Boy Scout Troop 1021 in Sturgeon Bay and the girls of troop 4011 who assembled and helped deliver them. If you know of a place where there isn't one yet, I have 43 empties with me tonight."

"So how much did we collect so far?" Amber Cross from Second Chances Thrift Shop called out.

"I was getting to that," Beth said laughing. "As of two hours ago, with the pancake breakfast, bake sale, and corndog sale included, we are just over $35,900."

Cheers and whistles accompanied even louder applause. Calls of "way to go, Beth" also came through the din.

Beth blushed and looked over to the picnic table where Marcus and the others were sitting. Marcus smiled and gave Beth two thumbs up. Beth took a deep breath and blew it out, relieved to know all her work had paid off and was appreciated. The amount was far from the needed millions, but at least it was a start, and judging from the enthusiasm and ever-growing crowds at these events, and not just due to the free food, Beth could see momentum was building.

"None of this would have been possible without all of you," Beth continued once the cheers died down, "Tomorrow is Bingo at the Baileys Harbor Town Hall at 6. Tickets are $5.00 a board, and there is no limit to the number of tickets you can buy for each round. There will be a bake sale and cash bar and something special planned for the last round."

"Now I would like to call Suzanne up here for a very special announcement," Beth called out, which started another round of applause as Suzanne Fish and Carol Wilson from Cheery Time Winery rose from their table and made their way to the front. Beth gave them both a quick hug before turning the microphone over to the ladies and headed to her table.

"I want to say that Beth has done a fantastic job organizing all these events," Suzanne began, "She has made our jobs very easy."

"And a hard act to follow," Carol said, leaning into the mic.

"After looking into many venues," Suzanne continued, "We are pleased to announce we have booked Northern Haus for our adult prom in August. We want this night to be truly a celebration of history, so, plan to dress in your finest attire from the year you graduated. We have also lined up stylists from Sturgeon Bay and Sister Bay who will be opening their salons to create period hair and make-up styles."

"If you are not the adventurous sort," Carol finished, "please come dressed to impress. We want to make the night an event to remember."

CHAPTER 34

"You've been awful quiet after the prom announcement," Marcus said, helping Beth load the now empty boxes and salad bowls into the backseat of the VW. "You should be so happy with your progress."

"I am," Beth replied.

"Your face says otherwise."

"It is nothing, really," Beth said, keeping her head down and pretending to be looking for something in the car in order for Marcus not to see the tears welling up in her eyes.

"Do you want to take a walk and shake off the 'nothing' that is bothering you."

"That would be nice," Beth admitted, wiping her eyes and standing up, being careful not to hit her head as she did so.

Marcus began to reach for Beth's hand but thought better of it and stuck both hands in his pockets.

They walked in silence for a few minutes, listening to the sounds of water lapping against the rocks. From one of the boats docked near the park, Beth could hear laughter and Marcus's name being called out. Marcus waved back towards the boat.

"You are popular around here," Beth commented.

"One of my recent repair jobs," Marcus said, "I also get called down to the docks quite often to bring my magnets and retrieve keys and bottle openers and other items people drop off their boats and into the water."

"So that is how you make your living, fixing porches and retrieving lost items."

"I'm never going to get rich doing odd jobs, but I like it. Besides, it gives me time to spend with Aaron," Marcus said thoughtfully. "I spent so many years when he was growing up caring for his mother, I feel like I missed so much, and now I think he resents me for it."

Beth stopped walking and sat on a large rock lining the water. Marcus picked up a handful of rocks and attempted to send them skipping across the surface of the water. Beth watched in amusement as the rocks hit the water and sank before even skipping once.

"Let me show you how it is done," Beth said, finding three smooth rocks of her own.

"You have to have smooth flat rocks, like this."

Beth placed the first rock on top of her middle finger and placed her thumb on top, holding it firmly in place. She used her index finger to spin the rock, sending it skipping six times across the surface of the water.

"Where did you learn to do that?" Marcus said, his mouth hanging open in surprise.

"There isn't much to do growing up in the middle of nowhere," Beth said. "Annie and I did our fair share of rock skipping at the reservoir."

"Was it hard?" Marcus asked, unsuccessfully attempting another skipped stone, "Growing up without a mother."

Noting Beth's silence at the question, Marcus reached out his hand, intending to rest it on Beth's, but he pulled back.

Beth sighed before answering.

"I think it was harder losing both my mom and my dad at the same time," Beth said. "I had Annie and her family, which helped."

"I can't shake the feeling that Aaron is slipping further away from me," Marcus said. "He was definitely his mother's son."

"He is seventeen," Beth said, "Do you remember what you were like at his age?"

"I was working at the Dairy Queen in Sturgeon every summer earning money for my truck and saving for college. I have no clue what Aaron wants to do, and he likes running off with his friends more than he likes working. I am honestly surprised he is holding his job at the mini golf this long."

"Things are very different from when we were young," Beth said, "But I can tell Aaron looks up to you. It shows by how much he watches you when you are together."

"I hope you are right."

"Speaking of Aaron, I thought he would be here tonight," Beth said, looking around the park, "I know how much he loves Edna's potato salad."

"He had the night off and was meeting some friends. He should be home by now, though," Marcus said, looking at his watch.

"I should be getting myself back as well," Beth said, "I was never a morning person before I came here, and 5:00 comes early."

"And you have your weekly Annie call to make," Marcus said as he stood up, wiping sand off the seat of his pants.

"Thank you for the walk," Beth said, taking the hand Marcus held out to help her up off the rock. "And thank you for not asking about my 'nothing really.'"

Marcus bent down to pick up another pair of smooth rocks. By the time he stood up, Beth was halfway to her car already. Marcus put the rocks in the back pocket of his shorts and sprinted off after her, arriving at her car in time to open the door for her.

Beth smiled, started the car, and drove in the direction of the Inn.

CHAPTER 35

Edna was already in bed when Beth returned home from the picnic. The growl in her stomach made Beth realize she had been talking so much at the picnic she really hadn't had a chance to eat more than a few bites. She made a plate of leftover potato salad, a brat without a homemade bun, and a slice of carrot cake from Pink Bakery. Balancing the plate in one hand and a bottle of root beer under her chin, she unlocked the door to her room just as her cell phone buzzed in her pocket. Setting the plate on the dresser, Beth glanced at the screen and saw it was Annie.

Beth clicked the answer and speaker buttons and set the phone on the table next to the window.

"Hi Annie," Beth said, changing out of her shorts and tank top and into her pajama's.

"You are early tonight. Is everything ok with you?"

"I am childless tonight," Annie answered back. "Darian took the boys to the movies, and the girls are at a sleepover. So, it is just me, a bottle of white paired with a box of mint girl scout cookies and blissful quiet."

"That sounds nice," Beth said, "I have had to spend the last few hours fielding questions about fundraising progress and avoiding becoming too close to Marcus again."

"So, no progress on the kiss event yet."

"He did bring Betty back to me, all repairs paid for."

"That's progress."

"And he made the effort to apologize without saying the words."

"More progress."

"But then I said something, or rather did not say something, and I may have set the progress back again," Beth admitted.

"It can't be all that bad," Annie said, "Can it?"

Beth sighed before answering Annie's question.

"We were talking about the adult prom we have planned, and Carol said the attendees should 'dress to impress'. I swear I heard Terry's voice saying those words in my head."

"What did you do?"

"When Marcus noticed I was very quiet, I told him it was nothing really and left it at that."

Beth paused and took a sip of root beer, wishing it was some of the wine Annie was enjoying.

"So, the 'nothin' really was really somethin'?" Annie asked.

"Yes," Beth answered, "I didn't want to tell Marcus because I was not sure how to. How do I tell the man who has been nothing but kind to me that three simple words can remind me of how I let someone have such control over me that he even told me what to wear and when. How do I tell him that, for twenty years, I was so weak?"

"You were not and never have been weak," Annie shot back. "Terry was just that much of a master manipulator and self-centered. It was always all about him."

"Did I tell you he called me this week twice?" Beth said.

"What'd he say?"

"I never answered," Beth replied, "And he never left a message. I have no idea what I would say to him if I did pick up."

"I know what you don't say. You don't say sorry and, for as much as I'd like you to, you don't come back."

Beth took another fork full of potato salad and a drink of soda.

"I wish you were here," Beth said, after a beat. "I need my best friend."

"I'm just a phone call away," Annie replied.

"It is not the same, but I know."

"Maybe I will fly up for this prom of yours."

"I'd like that."

The phone rang on Annie's side of the line.

"I gotta go," Annie said, "Gracie's messagin' SOS from her friend's house."

"Let me know if it is a giant spider again like last time," Beth said, laughing.

"I will." Annie replied, "Call you after the emergency is solved."

"I love you, you know," Beth said.

"I know."

Beth hung up the phone and placed it on the dresser. Grabbing an oversized towel from the drawer, she went into the bathroom and turned on the water to fill the claw foot tub. A cool breeze blew the curtain in the bathroom, and Beth took in a deep breath watching the tub fill. Samantha had stopped at the Lavender shop earlier in the week, so Beth poured some of the floral scented liquid into the tub and watched the bubbles form in the tub. When the tub was full, she stepped in and allowed the warm water and lavender to relax her sore muscles.

The clock in the bedroom struck midnight. Her bathwater was lukewarm when she left the tub and wrapped the soft towel around her body. Drinking the last sips of root beer, which was now nearly as warm as the bath she had just left, Beth released the towel and climbed into bed.

She knew there would be a great deal of work to do before Barb from the state historical society came on Tuesday, but that was a problem and chore for tomorrow.

CHAPTER 36

Beth blinked open her eyes, afraid she had overslept, and looked at the clock: 2:00.

Becoming more aware of the room, Beth realized what most likely had jolted her awake.

"You didn't call. You didn't answer your phone," Marcus's raised voice echoed in the otherwise still night air, "And then you decide to roll in two hours after curfew, thinking I wouldn't hear you."

"I said I was sorry," Aaron yelled back. "We were at the beach having a bonfire, and I just lost track of time."

"And who are the 'we'?"

"Just a couple girls we met swimming!"

"That's not what I asked you," Marcus said.

From her window, she was able to have a full view of Marcus' back yard. Beth could tell by the tone in his voice that Marcus was becoming angrier. This was the first time Beth had heard Marcus raise his voice to a volume louder than slight annoyance and never towards Aaron. She knew it was wrong to eavesdrop but couldn't pull herself away from the window.

"I was just with Stan and Joe from work. Then Wade and Kenny showed up, and we lost track of time."

"You know I don't like you hanging out with those boys; they are trouble. I can smell the cigarettes on your clothes."

"I wasn't smoking," Aaron replied, "Andy got there about an hour later with Mr. Carlson and brought us some stuff from the store, including cigarettes"

"Ross Carlson? What were you doing with him?"

"Nothing. He kept asking about the progress on the Sunset," Aaron replied, his voice starting to stutter and become quieter.

"What did you tell him?" Marcus replied, matching his son's tone.

"Nothing. I don't know anything. But he seemed real interested in how much we raised and the value of the land."

"And that's all?"

"Yeah, that's all. Once he showed up, the girls left with Joe and Stan," Aaron continued, "I got tired of being there when Carlson pulled out his stupid lighter and started flicking it like usual. Wade and Andy took him up on the cigarettes, but I didn't. Kenny drove me back to my truck, and that's when I realized I left my phone in the truck when I changed clothes. That's all."

"That's all?" Marcus asked, his voice back to its normal calm tones.

"Yes, dad," Aaron said, "That's all? I'm sorry."

"You know you still have to get up early for work," Marcus replied. "I should ground you for this."

"I know," Aaron replied with a tone which indicated he really was sorry. "I won't do it again."

"Yes, you will," Marcus said, with a small laugh, "You're a kid. I do remember what that was like, believe it or not. Now go to bed. We can talk more in the morning."

Beth watched as Marcus gave Aaron a quick hug before Aaron went into the backdoor of their house. She quickly ducked behind her curtains when she noticed Marcus looking up in her direction. Beth watched as Marcus retreated into the house, grateful she had not turned on the lights in her room.

CHAPTER 37

"B 12" Everett's voice boomed out, echoing from the stage at the Baileys Harbor Town Hall. The hall, built in 1930 with the library added in 1938, had seen more meetings, elections, craft shows, senior meals, and wedding receptions than could be counted. Tonight, it was housing approximately 200 bingo players working to raise money for the 'Save the Sunset' Preservation Fund.

"O 73," Everett called out. The microphone he used was not necessary in this hall; his voice would have worked just fine but added to the performance.

As a well-known host and MC for a large number of events in the county, Everett put on a show no matter what he was hosting, from trivia night to bowling banquets and even a stop at a child's lemonade stand. All were treated with the grandeur of the Oscar or Emmy Awards shows. Those who were privy to Everett's off-stage persona could attest to the fact that this was just his way. He took the time to get to know the county, the people in it, and the small, local businesses which gave Door County the reputation of a friendly and beautiful tourist destination. The fact he was friends with the owners and players of the Green Bay Packers football team and was known from time to time to talk one or two of the players and their wives to attend a local charity event didn't hurt his reputation locally either.

"G 55."

"Bingo" came the response from the back of the room.

"Come on up," Everett said, waving into the crowd, "Let's see if we have a winner."

Ruby Thompson, affectionately known throughout the county as 'the Bingo Granny' made her way up to the stage, her lucky bingo hat (she had a different one for every occasion) could be seen over the other players heads as she made her way through the tables. Everett took the card, which he knew would be a winner, and ceremoniously read off the numbers. As he announced a good bingo, the crowd politely applauded. Ruby proudly took back the winning card and a fresh package of lefsa bread from the winner's table and went back to her seat.

"We will now take a 20-minute break before the next round," Everett announced,

"And that round is the 50/50 charity round. Tonight's charity round will cost $10 a board with half the monies collected going to the lucky winner."

More applause.

"To make the benefit even better," Everett continued, "Fred Wickman from the Wickman House Resort and Bakery has agreed to match the charity winnings up to $7500 for the preservation and restoration of the Sunset Bar and Grill."

The applause and whistles at that announcement were even louder than before.

"So, be back here in 20 minutes. If you haven't purchased your bonus tickets yet, Marcie from the Wickman house and Tracy from the library will be coming around with cards, so hold up your hands if you need cards, and let's raise some money tonight."

Everett turned off the microphone and jumped off the stage rather than using the stairs. He wound his way through the crowded tables, taking time to shake hands and pat backs on his way to the refreshment area. Amy at concessions handed him an already open bottle of Spotted Cow, Everett's favorite next to Stubborn Sturgeon, and he continued his sweep through the crowd, stopping at the table where Beth and Aaron were sitting.

"Hey Aaron," Everett said with a smile, "How are you enjoying working the summer at Pirate's Cove? My daughter Amanda says you are a hard worker."

"It's ok," Aaron replied. "Though I'd like night shift better than mornings."

"More girls hanging around at night, I imagine," Everett replied, his grin growing even larger. Beth took a drink of her soda to stifle a laugh, noticing the blush which had begun to creep over Aaron's cheeks, visible even under the tan he had developed from working in the sun.

"I ain't much of a morning person," Aaron said with a stutter. "I think I need a break."

Aaron excused himself and made his way to the steps leading outside.

"You embarrassed him," Beth said, the smile still on her face, "I didn't think that was possible."

"You know he has a crush on my daughter Avery," Everett replied.

"I did not. I am going to have to save that little tidbit for a family dinner one night. I wonder if Marcus knows about this."

"Probably not." Everett took another drink of his beer and looked around the hall. "Speaking of Marcus, where is he? I was hoping to have him help with the bonus round donations. He always seems to sweet talk more tips out of the ladies."

"Come to think of it, I haven't seen him since the last break." Beth said, her smile switching to concern. "He became distracted suddenly and asked me to look after his cards. I thought he went to get another round of drinks."

Just like that, Marcus stepped up behind Beth.

"I thought I heard my name," Marcus said, putting his hand on the back of Beth's chair.

"We were just saying you skipped out on the last couple rounds," Beth replied.

The alarm on Everett's cell phone began to chime.

"All right everyone," Everett called out, grabbing his microphone again, "I hope we have sold enough in tickets and tips to make Fred write out a very large check."

Applause and cheers once again filled the hall as Fred Wickman waved his checkbook over his head.

"The first call for all the money is I 21."

"G 50. G Five Zero."

"Why do you keep looking out the window?" Beth asked, noticing the fact Marcus was distracted and not paying attention to his cards.

"I'm not sure," Marcus answered, "Something Aaron mentioned earlier got me thinking. Just now, he got in his car and drove off."

"Did you call him?"

"Yeah, it goes right to voicemail."

Everett continued to call out numbers as the sound of approaching sirens outside grew louder in the night air.

"That is a lot of sirens," Beth said, watching red and blue lights flash past the windows.

"Let's just keep playing," Everett said from the stage. "Most likely an accident further north. Nothing to be concerned about."

Even though he tried his best to keep the night light as he continued to call numbers, Everett couldn't help but feel uneasiness grow when the alarms at the neighboring fire station began to blare, and the firetruck sirens joined the others.

As the call of "Bingo" rose over the crowd, the downstairs door by the library clanged against the wall, and Chad Neuville ran into the room and over to Marcus and Beth's table. The look on Chad's eyes was a mix of panic and concern. As he bent over, still out of breath from his sprint up the stairs, to whisper in Marcus's ear, the emergency alert signal on Everett's phone and several other cell phones began to chime.

"Oh my gosh," Everett said, looking up into the crowd, eyes wide in panic and disbelief. "It's the Sunset," he said, his voice shaking, "The Sunset's on fire."

CHAPTER 38

The acrid smell of smoke filled the still air as Marcus and Beth parked on the side of the road behind the Sister Bay Fire Department Truck. Only three trucks of workers remained at the scene, checking for hot spots and working on clean-up, this one, a ladder truck from Ellison Bay, and the small tender from Sturgeon Bay. Chief Ridley pulled in with his own car and parked behind Marcus. The dark circles and drooping eye lids gave Beth the impression he had been on the scene most of the night and had managed to go back to the station only for a quick shower and change of clothes. The only other vehicles in the vicinity were Chad's SUV, the van from the radio station, a Channel 26 news van from Green Bay where the camera man and reporter were filming the scene, and two unmarked cars blocking traffic on either end of the fire zone.

Beth coughed as the bitter air caught in her throat. She took a drink from one of the bottles of water Edna had packed in the ice chest before offering bottles to the remaining firefighters.

"So, what do you know so far?" Marcus asked as Chief Ridley approached the truck.

"Not much yet," the chief replied. "The fire investigator will be here shortly. The electricity has been off for over three months and there has been no gas or propane tanks around the property for longer than that. Given the calm weather and remote location, it is doubtful a rogue spark from a campfire could have drifted over."

"So, what are you saying?" Marcus asked, putting his hand on the chief's back and leading him away from Beth and the other firefighters and even further from the earshot of the reporter. "Are you suggesting this was arson?"

"I am not saying anything," Ridley answered softly. "I am not saying anything or ruling anything out until after the fire inspector gets here."

"Chief," one of the firefighters called from the burned rubble of what had been a picnic table. "I have something to show you."

Chief Ripley excused himself and headed towards what was left of the Sunset.

"This isn't exactly how I wanted you to see the building we were trying to save," Marcus said to Beth when she approached, "Not much of anything to look at now."

Thinking of the pictures Chris had submitted for the collection canisters, Beth stared thoughtfully at the restaurant. The stone stairs and railings, now dirty with wet soot, still gave off the charm and welcome everyone at the preservation society had spoken so highly of. Even with the collapsed roof Beth could imagine the parties that had once been held within the walls.

"You look thoughtful," Marcus said, pulling Beth back to reality. "What are you thinking about?"

"I am trying to picture what this place was in its prime," Beth replied.

"Well, the restoration and the chance of being a historical landmark are pretty much a moot point now."

As if reading his mind, Marcus' cell phone buzzed.

"It's Fred," Marcus said, looking at the screen. "I was wondering when he would call."

Marcus stepped closer to the road, his voice low, the words undistinguishable.

Beth walked closer towards the burned-out Sunset.

"That area isn't safe yet, miss," one of the firefighters called in Beth's direction.

Beth stepped back, still scanning what was left of the restaurant.

"They are setting a 10: 00 meeting at Husby's to discuss what to do next," Marcus said, coming up behind Beth and putting his hand on her shoulder. "There is nothing we can do here now. I'm sure Edna could use your help with something at the Inn."

Driving away, Beth took one last look in the direction of the Sunset. The uncomfortable sadness sank in as she wondered if all her acceptance she had built up would now be as moot as the restoration she had been working on.

Marcus slowed as he approached his turn from Beach Road onto Porcupine Bay Road. With the roadblocks and detour signs, there was little traffic in the area, so seeing another car turn towards them was out of place. As the car passed, Beth clearly recognized the driver as Ross Carlson and Barb from the state historical society in the passenger side.

"What the…" Marcus muttered, recognizing the pair as well.

Beth turned her head around watching the car. As she did so, she noted Marcus was also following the car's progress in the rearview mirror.

CHAPTER 39

In sharp contrast to the picnic on Sunday, the atmosphere in the bar was somber and quiet. In the sparse gathering, Beth was able to pick out Fred Wickman, Chad and Abby, and Todd. David was pulled up to a table with Mrs. Wilson and Mrs. Thompson. This surprised Beth considering the ladies hadn't shown up for any meetings since the gathering at Marcus' house.

"Would you care for a drink?" Dotty asked from behind the bar. "You look like you could use something."

"Just a root beer, please," Beth replied, then went back to scanning the group, attempting find more familiar faces.

Spotting Chief Ripley at a corner table talking to a pair of unfamiliar men in suits and a younger woman wearing a blue jacket with CFI in white letters on the back, an uncomfortable feeling came over her. Spread on the table between the four were papers and legal pads full of notes. Barb Rescke came into the bar, and after a moment of searching, headed over to the table and pulled up a chair next to Chief Ripley who began to go through the papers, sharing some with Barb and putting others face down on the table between them.

Beth looked up when she heard the front screen door open as Marcus and Edna came in. She waved the pair, asking them to come sit with her. Shortly after, Chad and Abby joined them as well.

"Is there any more news?" Marcus asked, pulling out the chair for Edna so she could sit.

"No one has really said much," Chad answered, "I think everyone is still in shock."

"How bad is it?" Todd asked, pulling up a chair. "Can anything be saved?'

"We weren't allowed to see much this morning," Marcus said. "Too many hot spots and not much of the wreckage had been cleared yet. I wonder what they saw?" he continued, indicating the back table.

"Judging by the looks being exchanged," Chad said, "It can't be very good."

"All right everyone," Fred Wickman called out. "I think we should get started so we can be out of here before the lunch rush comes in. I think most of you know Chief Ripley. We also have Adam Mason, Ken Cross, and Angela Betts from Madison here with us."

The trio sitting with Chief Ripley raised their hands as their names were called.

"They are here to go over the property and building of the Sunset Bar and Grill and determine what caused the fire and if anything can be saved. They will be up here for a few days and are willing to answer the questions they are allowed to answer since this is potentially a legal matter."

"So, this was an arson fire?" David asked.

"It's too early to determine anything," Ridley answered.

"We did a preliminary walk through only this morning," Ken Cross added. "Ms. Betts just arrived an hour ago and will be using her expertise to go over the scene when we are told it is stable enough to enter the building."

"It's just that there have been a few restaurant fires up here the past few years," Fred said. "There was Mr. G's, which was arson, and Rowley's Bay. Not to mention the barn fire at the farm market. So, you can see why we are a bit nervous up here."

"As I said," Ripley responded, "we are looking into all possible causes of this fire and will know soon. When we find out, you will be told."

"So, what are we supposed to do now?" Mrs. Wilson asked. "How will this affect the sale of the property?"

"And the historical landmark process?" Mrs. Thompson added.

"I will let Barb Rescke answer those questions," Ken Cross said, motioning in Barb's direction.

"Unfortunately, I don't have good news on that front," Barb said standing up. "If a property has been declared a landmark, that designation would be removed. In this case, because the property was up for review only and the case closed, the building and the land go back to simply being a piece of property. Nothing more can be done for about that."

"Now what do we do?" Beth asked, "We raised a great deal of money for this property. We can't refund it."

"The property can still be sold," Barb said, "I have no say in what goes on once I file the forms with the state. I do know there are at least one or two other parties I have spoken with who are interested in the land, with or without a building."

"I wonder who that could be," Marcus said under his breath.

"My opinion," Barb continued. "Is that you should talk amongst yourselves and decide what your next move will be. Get a new estimate of the cost for the property and go from there."

"Well, I guess there isn't much more to discuss," Fred said with a shrug. "Why don't we all go home, think about our options, and meet again Sunday night. You're place again at 7, Marcus?"

Marcus nodded in agreement.

Defeat was on the faces of those gathered as they paid their tabs at the bar and filed out the doors. Marcus held out an arm for Edna who accepted the courtesy even though it wasn't needed.

"See you back home, sweetie," Edna said to Beth as they made their way to the exit.

Stepping out from the dim bar, Beth squinted against the bright sunlight. As she said goodbye to Abby, she noticed Ross Carlson standing just off the steps, nervously tapping his hands on his thighs, watching her leave. She made a mental note to tell Marcus this bit of information when she saw him. Backing out of the parking space, Beth noticed Barb Rescke exit the bar with the others who had been sitting at Chief Ripley's table. They casually shook hands, and Barb joined Ross in his car, and they drove north out of Sister Bay.

CHAPTER 40

Beth sat cross-legged at the picnic table watching the bubbles in her soda rise and pop at the surface of her glass. The sound of soft jazz music drifted on the air from the side porch where the guests staying in the Lilac Room were playing Scrabble. Beth closed her eyes thinking about the past few days.

"Penny for your thoughts," Edna said, coming up being Beth with a bucket of fresh picked cherries in one hand and a pair of empty bowls in the other hand. "It looks like you could use a distraction."

Beth sighed, taking the bucket and placing it on the table. She slid off the table and stood up, stretching her stiff muscles.

Edna took off one of the two aprons she was wearing and handed it to Beth and sat down on the bench across from her. Taking a pair of chopsticks out of her pocket, Edna handed one to Beth, then proceeded to take the stem off a cherry, poke the thin end of the chopstick into the cherry, and pop the pit out the other side in one quick movement. Beth picked up a cherry and attempted to do the same.

"You'll get the hang of it," Edna said, taking the slightly mangled cherry and popping the pit out with her knife. "The cherry doesn't have to look pretty in the scones. It just has to taste good."

After five or six more tries, Beth was nearly as proficient at cherry pitting as Edna—and at hiding her failed attempts by eating them.

"Do you remember the first time you said that to me?" Beth asked, setting down her chopstick and wiping her hands on her apron.

"You been here for only two weeks," Edna replied. "You had never hulled a strawberry or made fresh bread."

"I was also very much a stranger here, running to or from something. I wasn't sure which."

"And did you find the answer?" Edna asked.

"I thought I had, or at least I was starting to. I thought if I could find something to put all my effort into, I could start over. Working with these people towards a common goal was almost taking me there. Listening to all the stories, the history of that place, it made me wish I could have experienced the Sunset like all of you did. Then it was gone; in one night the magic was broken."

"The buildings may be gone, but the memories are still here. The stories we tell. The photographs we look back on. Everything changes. It's all a matter of looking at what is broken and deciding if those broken pieces are worth repairing or need replacing."

"How do you know which one to choose?" Beth asked, her hand instinctively reaching up to the chain around her neck.

"You trust, my dear," Edna said, reaching up and stroking Beth's hair. "You trust in yourself. That's what always worked for me."

She reached around and gently took the hand Beth was using to still hold her necklace and pulled the rings out from under Beth's top. "You trust yourself and follow your heart. And you hold tight to those who care about you."

Beth looked up at Edna, matching her smile, and closed her eyes, knowing the conversation was no longer about the Sunset.

It was at that moment the gate in the back yard slammed open against the fence.

"Beth, Edna," Marcus shouted, coming through the gate, "No one wanted to wait. It's unanimous."

"What are you talking about?" Beth asked, turning in Marcus' direction and noting the smile on his face.

"The committee, they are not waiting until Sunday," he said, "The plan to purchase is still on."

"You mean?"

"Yes," Marcus said, giving both Beth and Edna a hug at the same time. "And you, Beth, have a party to finish planning. Get your dancing shoes ready ladies, we're going to a prom."

CHAPTER 41

"How much more shopping is there?" Aaron asked, the annoyance in his voice not hidden since the third time he asked the same question an hour ago.

"Flowers? Check," Beth said, reading off her list. "Table covers and placemats?"

"Check and check," Abby answered looking at her list.

"Candles counted and loaded into the truck," Beth said.

"Where's my dad?" Aaron asked, looking at his watch.

"He said he had one last thing to pick up," Beth replied. "If you have everything in the truck, you are free to take it up north and start setting up. David and Mrs. Miller are waiting as well as the staff at Northern Haus. They said they would be there by noon. I know this must be boring for you."

"Yeah, whatever," Aaron said, fishing his keys out of his pocket. As he did so, a dirty gold lighter fell out of his pocket, and Aaron quickly bent down to retrieve it.

"I thought you said you weren't smoking?" Beth said. "You told your dad…"

"It's none of your business if I am or not," Aaron shot back. "Come on Abby, let's go."

Aaron gave one last glare in Beth's direction. There was something else besides anger in his eyes, but Beth could not tell exactly what it was.

"Well, it looks like it is just you and me again," Marcus said, walking up behind Beth and watching the truck leave. "What's his issue?"

"Besides being seventeen and stuck party shopping?" Beth replied. "Isn't that enough?"

"I suppose it is," Marcus said. "We have some time; did you want to get a bite to eat? You never know how busy we will be at the party."

"You pick the place," Beth said. "Surprise me."

"Where's your car?"

Beth looked up and down 3rd Avenue.

"Somewhere between the candy store, the big bookstore where we picked up Abby's new puzzles, and the store with the cats in it." Beth said, trying to remember.

"Sounds like Abby took you to all her favorite places."

"Shopping for comic books was the only time I think Aaron was happy."

"Sounds about right," Marcus said, taking Beth's hand and leading her down the street.

"By the way," Beth asked. "Where did you sneak off while I was shopping?"

"You'll see," Marcus said with a smile, spotting the familiar yellow VW Bug parked in front of Park Place Mall.

His smile turned into confusion, and he dropped Beth's hand.

"What the…?" he asked quietly, seeing a large brown mailing tube attached to the windshield wiper of the car with a heavy rubber band. He picked up the tube, turning it over in his hands. There was no label or writing to indicate where it came from or who had left it on Beth's car.

"What is it?" Beth asked, looking around Marcus' back at the envelope.

Marcus pulled off the white cap holding the tube closed and pulled out several large pieces of yellowed paper. He opened the first layer and laid it on the front of the car. On the paper was the blueprint sketch of the original layout of the Sunset Bar and Grill with the name Resting Sun written in perfect script. The second page was the addition of the kitchen expansion. Each page Marcus pulled back showed more and more of the improvements made to the buildings, with the last a hand drawn sketch of the finished Sunset.

"Where did these come from?" Beth asked.

"It doesn't say," Marcus answered, carefully rolling the pages back together and inserting them into the tube. "But I'll try and find out."

CHAPTER 42

Beth stood in front of the full-length mirror in her room and recalled the last time she had seen herself in this dress. The black sequins glittered in the light with every movement. The waist was a bit tighter than she remembered, but the side zipper closed, and she was able to breathe. "Eating may be a different story," Beth thought to herself. The tan she had developed over the summer gave her a healthy glow, and she smiled at her reflection as she put her earrings in. Her one regret was not having Annie here to give her support.

A soft knock on the door brought Beth's thoughts back to the present.

Beth opened her bedroom door, expecting to find Samantha or Edna waiting to take her to the party. She knew Marcus and Aaron would already be at the location, and the ladies had made plans to go together. She also knew Edna had included a free night to each guest who bought a ticket to the prom, so the Inn was officially empty during party time. Even baby Lynette was going to be dressed and in attendance. Beth looked up and down the hall before noticing the oblong blue velvet box on the rug in front of her door. She picked up the box, still scanning the hallway and backed up into her room.

The note attached to the box simply stated, "This is your night."

The black and grey crystal choker in the box sparkled against the white cushion in the box. Beth's hands shook as she held the necklace against her skin and attempted to work the clasp. After the third try, the choker fell into place. The colors matched her dress perfectly, as if it was meant to be all along. Beth ran her fingers across the beads, admiring how they looked in the mirror. As she turned to pick her clutch off the dresser, her smile disappeared, and she felt a wave of sadness. Peeking out from under the choker was the thin gold chain holding her wedding rings.

Beth held up the chain and stared at her reflection in the mirror. Still shaking, Beth unhooked the clasp and placed the necklace and the rings on the dresser in front of her.

With a deep sigh and a final glance, Beth headed towards the door

CHAPTER 43

The parking lot at Northern Haus was three-quarters full when Beth pulled into the spot Marcus had reserved for her near the main doors. She recognized many of the cars from town in the parking lot, but there was also a great many Illinois, and Minnesota license plates mixed in as well. Marcus' truck was near the side door alongside Aaron's. Samantha had driven up with Edna, and Chad had driven the sheriff car in. It was conveniently parked facing out next to the driveway. She also noticed, with a mix of surprise and annoyance, Ross Carlson's red Escalade parked in the lot.

The front doors were wide open, and Beth could hear lively 70's disco music before she made it to the entrance. Todd and Andrew from the bakery were just inside the doors, talking on their phones. Beth smiled at them as she walked in.

"Beth, you look awesome," Abby called out, running up and giving Beth a tight hug. Even though this was an adult prom, Abby and Angel had been allowed to come, as well as Aaron and a few other teens who would be helping with the photo booth, raffle, and food service so their parents could enjoy the party.

"Look at you all dressed up," Beth replied, as Abby twirled, showing off her burgundy and gold gown, the tulle underneath billowing out as she turned, highlighting the glitter in the skirt. "I think this is the first time I have seen you in anything other than jeans."

"I must say, you clean up quite nicely yourself," Marcus said, coming up behind Abby.

"You look very sharp yourself," Beth replied, admiring Marcus' navy-blue tuxedo complete with shiny jacquard fabric blazer and matching cummerbund and bow tie.

"You wore that to prom?"

"With matching socks," Marcus admitted. "May I?"

Marcus extended a hand and offered to lead Beth to the main dance floor.

The dance floor was half full of couples and singles and even a few groups dancing and laughing. Tulle banners draped from the ceiling were highlighted by silver disco balls, gold glitter stars, and white fairy lights. Battery operated candles flickered on royal, blue-covered tables scattered around the room. The action around the punch and cupcake table was brisk and constant, keeping the students who were helping busy, and, judging by the smiles on their faces, as happy as the partygoers.

The music switched from disco to polka, and the dancers on the floor switched as well. The line at the punch table grew longer as those leaving the dance floor sought out refreshments or wandered in the direction of the silent auction tables.

"So, have you bid on the signed Packer football yet?" Beth asked Marcus when they finished at the photo booth. She knew he had been eyeing it up since the box came in the mail last week.

"And the jacket," Marcus replied.

"But I outbid him," Chad said, coming around the corner of the table. "You look lovely tonight, Beth."

"I see you went all out tonight, too," Beth said with a laugh, noting the tuxedo print t-shirt worn over brown uniform pants.

"I am, unfortunately, on duty, and I needed something my jacket would fit over," Chad replied.

"Punch anyone?" David asked, rolling up with a tray of plastic cups filled with sparkling orange liquid and Chris pushing his chair.

"Smells wonderful," Beth said, taking a glass, "what is it?"

"Pineapple juice, mango juice, and orange sherbert mixed with lemon-lime soda," Chris replied, handing a glass to Chad. "Don't worry, it's not spiked like someone did at our prom. Right, Marcus?"

"I don't remember that," Marcus said in mock disbelief.

"He really was a prankster in high school," Chad said.

"That I can believe," Beth said, "I have seen a few hints of trouble since I have known him."

"Before Chad tells you any more lies about me," Marcus said, taking Beth's hand and leading her to the side table of auction items.

"I think we should see how much more I have to add to my winning football bid."

"We'll see about that," Chad called after them.

Beth hadn't seen all the items up for bid since Mrs. Wilson had volunteered to oversee that aspect of the evening. Marcus added another $50 to his football and jacket bids, and Beth chose to add her name to the selection of books donated by Write On Door County which featured ten autographed books by local authors. She also added an amount to the gift certificate from the Ice Cream Factory and other restaurants with full intention of giving the ice cream to Marcus if she won.

"I have to excuse myself," Marcus said, touching Beth gently on the shoulder, "I seem to be needed at the photo booth. Something about a loose curtain to fix."

"I will be right here," Beth said, as she watched Marcus disappear into the crowd.

"You have really assembled quite a show here, haven't you?"

Beth turned around and found herself face to face with Ross Carlson.

"Don't worry, I come in peace," Ross said, noting the questioning look on Beth's face. "I figured this was as good a time as any to check in on your progress for the preservation effort, since I clearly see that it is still on."

"Yes, it is, Mr. Carlson," Beth replied quickly.

"Please, call me Ross. May I ask you for a dance?" Ross asked as the rock music switched to a slower dance tune.

Beth reluctantly agreed, not wanting to be impolite. Also, she was curious about what the developer was really up to.

"You don't like me much, do you?" Ross asked, putting his hand carefully on Beth's waist.

"I don't really know you enough to make that decision," Beth replied.

"I am sure you have heard stories."

"I have."

"And still you agreed to this dance."

"Mr. Carlson," Beth began.

"Ross."

"Ross," Beth continued, "I have learned to make my own decisions on whether to speak, or dance, with someone."

"Thank you for that," Ross said with a nod, "Now, what do you hear about the fate of the Sunset?"

"You tell me," Beth replied, "I seem to recall seeing you with the state historical representative several times."

"By request of Ruth Dickerson in fact," Ross answered. "I think they both felt I would know more of the value of her property than anyone in the preservation committee."

"And I am sure it had nothing to do with your family wanting to purchase the land and build on it."

"I am certain that is what everyone is thinking, but I can assure you, I want this sale to go smoothly and by the book without any misconceptions or preconceived notions."

"And what about the fire?" Beth asked.

"That was a tragedy," Ross answered, "The Sunset is, was, a beautiful building. Well-designed to fit into its backdrop. There was history there."

Beth noticed a shift in Ross' demeanor as he talked about the fire, almost regret or loss.

"When I told Ruth about the fire, she was devastated, poor thing," Ross continued. "The Sunset is, was, her life. She asked me to call her attorney to help 'get her affairs into order,' she said."

"I'm sure she did," Marcus said, coming up behind Ross and placing his hand on his shoulder. Beth noticed the tone of anger in Marcus' voice.

"I can see where I am not wanted," Ross said, stepping back and allowing Marcus to stand closer to Beth. "Thank you for the dance. You really did put quite a nice party together here."

Marcus turned and watched as Ross moved towards the food table and disappeared into the crowd. Marcus also noticed that others were also watching the developer leave, most likely wondering, as he was, why Ross had come.

"What did he want?" Marcus asked, turning his attention back to Beth who had also been watching the man leave.

"He was asking how much progress we were making," Beth replied. "He was rather pleasant, actually."

"I do not trust him or his family," Marcus said, looking back in the direction Ross had walked away in. "I can't help thinking there is something up with him."

"I think you worry too much," Beth said. "I also think I would like to have a dance with you."

"If that is what the lady wishes," Marcus said with a bow. "That is what my lady will get."

Beth relaxed her shoulders, feeling Marcus' hand gently rest on her waist while his fingers twined with hers. She looked up into his eyes and smiled, as they smoothly turned in step as Elvis Presley crooned, 'Wise men say, only fools rush in', in the background.

CHAPTER 44

"What's the matter?" Marcus asked, coming up behind Beth who was resting her head on the pillar of the back porch. "Your party and you were a big hit tonight."

"I know," Beth replied. "Even Mr. O'Hern got up the nerve to ask Edna for a dance. And old Mrs. Wilson and Mrs. Thompson got into the chicken dance."

"And the conga line," Marcus said, laughing.

"I hope someone was kind enough to help old Mr. Lawrence home, or I am afraid the goats might not be the only things sleeping on Al Johnson's roof in the morning."

Beth smiled, but there was still a sadness behind the grin.

"I suppose you are going to need to return this," Beth said, reaching up to unclasp her necklace. "It was very sweet of you..."

Marcus put his hand over Beth's, stopping her.

"I bought that for you," he said, "It's yours. You deserve something nice for all the work you have been doing here. Now, what is wrong?"

"I don't know. I guess I am being paranoid or something. I mean, everyone has been so good to me. Edna took me in. You forgave me for giving your yard a new look. The people have been wonderful and accepting. I keep waiting for the other shoe to fall."

"The clock has already struck midnight, and you are still here," Marcus said. "And I am still here."

"I wonder though, since the plans for the Sunset are finished, if I will go back to just being a tourist again," Beth said, swallowing back tears. "I feel like if my name doesn't end with 'son', I'm just a foreigner."

"I have been here since I was two," Marcus said, putting his hand on Beth's shoulder. "And I feel that way once in a while. Stick around long enough, and it gets better."

"Is that an invitation?" Beth asked cautiously.

"No. I mean, yes," Marcus stammered, "But only if you want it to be."

CHAPTER 45

"What time is it?" Beth asked as she picked up her phone from the pillow next to her.

"It's nearly 6:15," Marcus said.

"That's too early to be up," Beth complained, rolling over and wiping the sleep from her eyes.

"You are up this early every day for Edna," Marcus said with a laugh. "What makes today so different?"

"I'm usually not awake talking until 2 a.m," Beth said, slipping out of bed and pulling a fresh pair of jeans and t-shirt from the closet. "And why are you up so early?"

"I promised Father Fox I would go down today with Jimmy to Milwaukee and pick up the lumber for the new graveyard fencing. We are leaving early and getting the wood and then the new headstones from Madison. I'll be back tomorrow afternoon."

"Give me five minutes, and I will be over with fresh scones," Beth said, putting on her sandals and running down the steps.

Marcus was waiting by his back porch with a large mug of steaming coffee when Beth came through the fence connecting the yards.

"Are you sure you have to leave this early?" Beth said, handing Marcus the basket of warm scones and taking the mug in her other hand.

"I promised I would get this errand done this week."

Beth opened her mouth to protest some more, but the ring of Marcus' cellphone stopped her. She took a sip of coffee and followed Marcus into the kitchen. She couldn't hear the conversation, but by the animated movements of his arms and his pacing, she could tell something was wrong.

Marcus hung up the phone and leaned against the counter with his eyes closed.

"What is it?" Beth asked, coming up behind him and touching him on the back.

"Tell me again what Ross Carlson was talking about last night at the party?"

"Nothing, really," Beth answered. "He wanted to know about the funding for the Sunset preservation."

"Did you happen to notice if he had his ever present lighter with him?"

Beth took a minute to think.

"Honestly, no," Beth said, "Come to think of it, I didn't see him with the lighter when he was at Husby's either."

"Hmm, Ok," Marcus said, staring blankly at the kitchen wall.

"What is up?" Beth asked, "Who was that on the phone?"

"That was Chad. They arrested Ross Carlson last night. He's being charged with arson in the case of the Sunset Bar and Grill."

Beth stood up straight, trying to absorb what Marcus had just said.

"What happens now?" Beth asked.

"I'm not sure," Marcus said. "I imagine there will be a hearing and the courts involved."

"So, everything will have to be put on hold?"

"Most likely for now. Chad didn't say much, just that Ross was arrested. This is a small community. I am sure you will hear more soon."

"But for now, we wait?" Beth asked.

"You wait here. I need to drive to Milwaukee," Marcus said, bending down to kiss Beth on the forehead. "Call me if you hear anything?"

"I'll call," Beth said. "I promise."

Marcus paused at the front door and turned to smile at Beth.

"Take care of yourself while I'm gone," he said, closing the door behind him.

"I'll miss you, too," Beth said, turning around.

Beth had not heard Aaron's bedroom door open, and she also was not sure how much of the conversations he had heard. Beth was aware of the look of shock on Aaron's face, and also aware of the look on his face as his shock turned to anger.

She opened her mouth to say something, but Aaron had already turned and ran out the back door. Beth winced as the door slammed shut, the wood rattling in the frame. She stood there listening as Aaron's truck started up and skidded on the rocks of the driveway.

CHAPTER 46

"Oh, Annie," Beth said rocking on the porch swing, Cleo curled comfortably in her lap,

"How can something be so good and so messed up at the same time?"

"Let me get this straight," Annie replied, "The good part is he kissed you again."

"Yes."

"And you shared a sunrise breakfast at his place."

"Until we were interrupted by a phone call," Beth replied. "And up until Aaron saw me in their kitchen and stormed out."

"He's a kid," Annie said, "He's gonna act like a kid if he sees somethin' he don't like."

"But we did not do…"

"I know, but Aaron doesn't know that," Annie cut in. "You were with his dad early in the morning. That's all a kid needs to see, 'specially' since you ain't his mom."

"Do I go look for him?"

"Beth, just let him be," Annie answered, "He needs to cool off. If my Calvin has taught me anythin' about a seventeen-year-old, it's that they come back home when they are broke or hungry. And don't you be callin' Marcus either. There's nothin' he can do."

Beth sat back on the swing, letting her head hit hard against the back, startling Cleo awake.

"I am so out of my league here," she said, moaning.

"Welcome to the world of teenagers," Annie replied. "I thought mine had taught you all about raisin' kids."

"At least with yours I was able to send them back to you."

"Now that we have the kiss and the kid figured out," Annie said, "what else is buggin' ya?"

"The whole fire business," Beth answered. "Something still feels off."

"How do ya mean?"

"It seems too easy. When I saw Ross at the dance, he seemed truly upset about the Sunset burning down, not like someone who knew the property could be bought cheaper or be easier to develop."

"Why do you say that?"

"There was something in his eyes," Beth said. "I felt sorry for him, too. Maybe I felt the kinship of two outsiders."

"Now that sounds like the Beth I know," Annie said laughing. "Always needin' to see the good in people."

"Even if there is no good to be found?"

"'Specially then," Annie replied, "It's what makes you, you."

"So, what do I do next?"

"Just roll with it and see where life takes ya'."

"I miss you to pieces, you know," Beth said.

"I miss you, too," Annie said. "I gotta go now. My next appointment's here."

Beth hung up the phone and sat back on the swing. Cleo rolled over on his back and began to purr as Beth rubbed his belly. Beth yawned in response to Cleo's yawn as the cat fell asleep on her lap. Closing her eyes, Beth rested her head on the swing back.

Her rest was short lived as Chad's sheriff car pulled to a fast stop in front of the house, and Chad ran up to the porch with only a few large strides.

"Beth," Chad called, a look of concern on his face. "You need to come with me. Aaron's been hurt."

"What?" Beth said, standing up, sending Cleo falling to the porch floor.

"It's Aaron," Chad repeated, "He's been in a fight."

CHAPTER 47

"They are going to be taking him to a room shortly," Chad said, handing Beth a tea from the vending machine. "I explained to the nurses that Marcus was out of town, and you were his girlfriend and as close to family Aaron has here right now."

"How bad is it?"

"Mostly bruises and cuts. He did have two cracked ribs from being kicked and there will be a good shiner," Chad replied.

Beth was listening to Chad explain Aaron's injuries but became distracted by the nurse coming towards them. Abby, who had been sitting quietly, sipping a soda, stood and put her hand in Beth's.

"Ms. Campbell?"

"Yes," Beth replied.

"We called Aaron's father and finally were able to speak with him. He gave us permission to share information since Aaron isn't awake yet."

"How is he?" Beth asked, squeezing Abby's hand.

"We gave him something for pain, so he is sleeping," the nurse answered. "He will be admitted for observation tonight since his father is still out of town. He is down for a head CT now and then going to his room. If you would like, you can wait there. But only one of you."

The nurse disappeared back behind the divider that separated them from the waiting area and the emergency room. Beth looked over at Chad.

"I will wait here with Abby," Chad said, "My wife is getting off duty soon anyway, and then she can take Abby home."

"Do you know who did this?" Beth asked.

"It was Wade Kole and Kenny Johnson."

"What? Why?"

"They are not talking. We had an anonymous tip that there was a fight by the quarry," Chad answered. "When we arrived, Aaron was on the ground, and we arrested the other two."

"And they are not saying anything?"

"Not without parents and a lawyer."

The nurse appeared again with a bag of Aaron's things.

"I can take you to his room to wait," the nurse said.

Beth gave Abby a tight hug.

"He is going to be fine," Beth said, seeing the tears in Abby's eyes. "I will watch over him until Marcus gets back."

Abby tried to fake a smile as best as she could before burying her face into her father's hip.

"Thank you for coming to get me," Beth told Chad.

"It was the least I could do for Marcus and Aaron," Chad answered. "These are the keys for Aaron's truck. We had it towed here."

"Thank you again," Beth said.

She gave Chad a quick hug and followed the nurse down the hall to the elevator.

CHAPTER 48

Beth rested on the seat under the window and stared out at the hospital parking lot. A pair of robins were flitting around the tree closest to the building, and several squirrels ran back and forth across the grass. The head nurse had come in to check on Aaron's IV about an hour earlier and offered Beth a menu. She had chosen the pork and mashed potatoes with steamed asparagus and applesauce. The cherry crumble was not as good as Edna's, but it was better than most hospital food, and Beth had finished everything on her tray.

Aaron was still asleep, as he had been since the radiology techs had brought him in over four hours ago. Doctor Kramer had come in and reported the CT had not shown any signs of a concussion, but they still wanted Aaron to stay overnight for observation. Beth had put her phone on speaker, allowing Marcus to hear the report. After the doctor had left, she stayed on the phone, reassuring Marcus and telling him not to rush and risk a speeding ticket.

Aaron moved in the bed, moaning and wincing in pain. Beth went to the side of the bed and pulled up the chair.

"Dad?" Aaron said, his voice a whisper.

"No, Aaron," Beth answered. "I'm here,"

Aaron attempted to turn his head and cried out in pain.

"Don't try to move," Beth said, straightening the pillow that had shifted behind Aaron's head.

"Where's my dad?"

"He's on his way back home tonight. He should be here in a few hours."

"Why are you here?" Aaron asked, coughing.

"You were hurt, and someone needs to be here."

"Why you?" Aaron asked, turning his head away from Beth.

"Because, like it or not, I care about you," Beth said.

Aaron shifted in the bed again but said nothing.

"You know this is going to be a very long couple hours if you don't want to talk to me," Beth said, breaking the silence.

Beth looked over at Aaron who had closed his eyes, pretending to be asleep.

Annie's words, "Let him come to you," echoed in Beth's ears. She picked up one of the books she had won at the silent auction and tried to read but was unable to concentrate. Beth went back to staring out the window and watching a red squirrel chase a blackbird across the parking lot.

"He didn't do it," Aaron said, his voice low and shaky.

"What?" Beth responded, setting down her book and going to the chair next to the bed.

"He didn't do it," Aaron repeated, "Mr. Carlson. He didn't start the fire."

Aaron closed his eyes again. It took extra self-control for Beth to not say anything, just wait. Aaron coughed and winced.

"I heard dad on the phone, and I wanted to tell him, but then I came out and saw you in our kitchen, in her kitchen, and I was mad," Aaron said, reaching for the cup of ice water on the bedside table, clumsily knocking it over. Beth reached for the cup and held the straw to Aaron's mouth,

"I just ran," Aaron continued after taking a sip of water and resting back against the pillows. "I drove to the quarry and called Wade. I told him to turn himself in. But he just laughed at me. He said they had already arrested Mr. Carlson. They found his lighter upstairs in the restaurant and the beer bottles with his fingerprints. But it was all a lie."

Aaron took another drink of water and looked up at Beth with a look of gratitude before speaking again.

"I told Wade and Kenny I would go to the police myself if they didn't. I would tell Mr. Neuville about the fireworks and the beer Wade stole from Mr. Carlson's garage, everything. Wade just laughed again and hit me. They just kept hitting and kicking. I tried to fight back, but they were too strong. I pretended to pass out, so they stopped. Next thing I knew I heard Wade's car drive off, and Andy was calling 911."

Maternal instinct took over and Beth reached over and took Aaron gently into her arms, hugging and rocking him. She felt him attempt to pull away, but gradually sank into her embrace, his face buried into her shoulder as he began to cry.

"It's ok," Beth said softly. "It's over now, and you are safe. Chad told me they arrested Wade and his friends."

"I'm sorry," Aaron said, taking a deep breath.

"There is nothing to be sorry about," Beth said, stroking Aaron's head. "You did the right thing."

"I'm sorry I was so mean to you," Aaron continued, removing himself from Beth's hug and settling back on the pillows, tears still in his eyes. He turned away and looked at the opposite wall. "I didn't want to like you. When I saw you in the kitchen, I wanted to scream at you to get out. That was mom's place, not yours."

"I can underst…"

"I'm not done yet," Aaron said, roughly cutting Beth off. "I was mad at you and dad, and I was mad at me. I thought, if I didn't like you, you would leave. But I saw how my dad looked at you, like how he used to look at my mom. I was afraid if I started to like you, I would be betraying my mom."

"I came here because I was running away from my life," Beth said after a brief silence, "I was in a bad place, and I was thinking of ending it all. But then I ran into your father's lawn. And your dad was gentle and kind and funny, and when he brought me into his world of saving something so special to him, I found a purpose. He told me how he met your mother at the Sunset when he was seventeen, and he was a prep cook, and she was a server."

"He told you that?" Aaron asked.

"He told me a lot about your mother and you," Beth answered. "No one can replace your mother, not in your heart or your dad's. But from what I learned about mom, I don't think she would want your dad growing old and lonely either."

"So, do you love him?"

"I don't know," Beth said, "But I know I really do like him—and you."

"Ms. Beth Campbell?"

Beth and Aaron both turn towards the man who had appeared in the doorway.

"Yes?" Beth replied.

"You are a hard person to track down," the man said, his face stern and unsmiling. "I have been instructed to give these to you."

Beth stood up to retrieve the two large envelopes the man held out to her. As soon as she took them and signed the form on the clipboard, he turned and disappeared down the hallway.

There was barely time to look at the address stamped on the envelope before Marcus rushed into the room and to Aaron's side.

"What happened?" Marcus asked, putting his arms around Aaron.

Beth tucked the envelopes under her jacket and gathered up the rest of her things.

"Tell your father what you told me," Beth said, "Everything is all right now."

Marcus looked up at Beth.

"Thank you," he said with a slight smile.

Beth nodded, returning the smile, and left the two alone in the room. She hesitated for a moment and listened as Aaron began telling Marcus about the fire and the fight.

CHAPTER 49

Beth sat on the stone steps of the Sunset staring out over the still water. A large ship, a thousand-footer, Marcus had told her, was slowly making its way down the bay towards the shipyard in Sturgeon Bay for cleaning and repairs. The unopened envelopes from the hospital sat in her lap. Beth did not hear the footsteps coming towards her from the back of the building.

"So, how's the boy?" Ross Carlson asked, wiping soot off the stone step and sitting down next to Beth.

Beth jumped slightly at the intrusion.

"His dad is with him now," she replied.

"I know he was the one who stood on my side and turned Wade and the other boys in. I'm not pressing charges for breaking into my garage, I think the bottle rockets and underage drinking will get them in enough trouble by itself."

"The sheriff said they had evidence against you," Beth said.

"Circumstantial and easily explained. I was here that day, earlier, just after the rain. My tire tracks were here because I was getting something out of the safe for Ruth. I must have dropped the lighter upstairs, but I have so many left over from my father's giveaways I didn't notice. I heard Wade and Kenny and a bunch of other kids down by the beach at their bonfire, so I left quickly. I heard them shooting off the fireworks. If I had stopped or reported it, then maybe… But not many people like me around here, so…" Ross stopped talking and looked out over the bay with Beth.

"I've noticed," Beth said, softly.

"Except for you," Ross replied, "And Aaron."

"What do you mean?" Beth asked, turning to look at Ross for the first time since he sat down.

"You didn't judge me," Ross said, "You even danced with me. And Aaron, he is a good but confused kid. I lost my mother when

I was about his age. Car accident. He has a good relationship with his father, unlike the one I had with mine."

"I'm not following," Beth said, wanting to know more. "I had the impression from the first time I saw you at Edna's that Aaron didn't like you very much."

"I thought so too," Ross replied, "Then I found out we had a second thing in common. Did you know Aaron is a great artist?"

"Marcus mentioned something about Aaron following in his mother's footsteps that way."

"I saw him out at Ellison Bluffs sketching, and we started talking. He said he wanted to be an architect and that he hated my building designs," Ross laughed slightly, "I told him so did I, but I did what the client wanted. We started meeting once a week at different locations to talk about his designs. He was the one that helped me get the Sunset plans on your car in Sturgeon Bay."

"That was you," Beth said, surprised.

"Did you know my great grandfather designed the summer kitchen and root cellar of the Sunset? He signed the plans."

"No, I didn't," Beth said, "does anyone else know that?"

"Ruth Dickerson did. That's why we have been talking. She likes me too, so I have three people on my side."

"You have to have more than that."

"Not really," Ross said. "The Carlson name isn't well liked. After my great grandfather died, he left the business to my grandfather, and all the money as well. By the time my father became involved, the estate was worth several million. He kept buying land and building on it without thinking. So, people resented him. He outbid and overbuilt."

"You don't sound happy about that," Beth replied.

"I'm not," Ross replied, "When he tore down the baseball diamond and the volleyball court where everyone played growing up, I left the company. So now I am trying to make the Carlson name something else, something better. And I want to start with this place," Ross said, indicating the Sunset and its properties.

"I see you haven't opened your other gift yet," Ross said, putting a hand on the envelopes on Beth's lap.

"These?" Beth asked, surprised.

"Open it."

Reluctantly Beth did as Ross asked. The cover page was from a law firm in Green Bay. Beth took a deep breath. There was also a handwritten envelope which read, 'Open first'. Beth opened the envelope and began to read the carefully handwritten letter.

To whom it may concern, I, Ruth Dickerson, upon my death, wish to donate the property known as the Sunset Bar and Grill to the Sunset Preservation Society. I have returned the original plans and blueprints over to Ross Carlson Designs, LLC. There is also a trust set up for building expenses with the intent of rebuilding. Enclosed in these envelopes are all the legal notices needed as outlined by my attorney.
Signed, Ruth Anne Dickerson

Beth turned the papers over in her hands, skimming the pages in disbelief.

"Did you have something to do with this?" Beth asked, glancing from papers to Ross and back again.

"I had to," Ross said, "I couldn't let my family outbid you. This place is too special to be destroyed by steel, concrete, and glass."

"Won't your family be angry with you?"

"Most likely," Ross said with a laugh, "But sometimes a person has to decide what is worth saving and what isn't. They need to figure out if starting over is worth fighting for."

Beth looked at Ruth's letter one last time before putting it back into the envelope.

She looked up, intending to say thank you to Ross, but he had already walked off behind the building and into the woods behind the Sunset.

CHAPTER 50

Beth stood staring out the window of her room watching the back yard lights flicker on, as did the porch light at Marcus' house. Somewhere there was a fire burning, and the scent of burning wood drifted across the yards. Canadian geese formed a lopsided V as they flew over the houses, a few landing in the back yard in search of the corn Edna had tossed out from the back porch.

Beth picked up the chain and rings from the side table where they had sat and ran her fingers across the familiar surface. It seemed oddly appropriated that the engraved 'Everlasting' had all but worn smooth with only the "e" and "s" somewhat visible.

She thought about the conversation with Ross and about what Edna had told her. "Sometimes a person has to decide what is worth saving and what isn't. They need to figure out if starting over is worth fighting for."

Beth took a big sigh, a habit she had all but broken in the past few months after arriving here and took another look at the rings in her hand.

She picked up her phone and dialed. The ringing was cut short by an all too familiar voice, not the usual answering machine.

"Hello, Terry," Beth said, slipping the rings in the drawer of the side table and closing the drawer. "We need to talk."

The End

ABOUT THE AUTHOR

Margaret Magle is a 40+ year transplant to Sturgeon Bay from Fond du Lac, WI. Inheriting her love of books and all things writing from her mother, Margaret has written several plays, poetry, short stories and is working on more books, including a sequel to Saving *the Sunset Bar and Grill*. With husband David, Margaret owns OtherWorlds Book & More. When not writing, she enjoys reading, making beaded jewelry, and snuggling her three cats.

www.ingramcontent.com/pod-product-compliance
Lightning Source LLC
Chambersburg PA
CBHW070759160726
48004CB00001B/254